Super Bowl

GEORGE VECSEY

SCHOLASTIC INC.
New York Toronto London Auckland Sydney

Cover photo: Focus on Sports.
Photo opposite page 74: Camera 5, Ken Regan.

ISBN 0-590-40451-2

12 11 10 9 8 7 6 5 4 3   7 8 9/8 0 1/9

Printed in the U.S.A.   01

To Marianne

CONTENTS

A Super Day

Late in the afternoon of January 26, 1986, a large young man named William (Refrigerator) Perry began running with the football during Super Bowl XX. Not only did Perry run with the ball, but he cranked his huge right arm as if he intended to pass. Most of the 73,818 fans in the Superdome in New Orleans leaned forward to watch history in the making. Across the country, millions more watched on their television screens.

This huge audience — to say nothing of the millions of other fans around the world — was watching Refrigerator Perry of the Chicago Bears expand his legend. During the 1985 season, he had gone from a much-maligned rookie defensive lineman to an occasional blocker and running back for the Bears. Now, in the Super Bowl, Perry was faking a forward pass against the New England Patriots. He was the largest man ever to run with the ball in the 20 years of the Super Bowl.

As it turned out, Perry thought better of passing, and was tackled for a loss, although later in Super Bowl XX he would rumble for a touchdown. The televison audience, estimated at 127 million, was the largest in television history, eclipsing the record of 121.6 million viewers who saw the final chapter of *M*A*S*H* on February 28, 1983.

For three hours on that Sunday afternoon, the United States, as well as many other countries around the world, practically stopped still for football. It proved once again that Super Bowl Sunday had become another American holiday.

There have been 20 Super Bowls, but Super Bowl XX has the distinction of being the most lopsided of them all. With both teams playing in their first Super Bowl, the Bears romped over the Patriots, 46–10.

Although the score was one-sided, most fans stayed in their seats or in front of their television sets until the end. The Patriots had their loyal supporters from New England; and the Bears, one of the most famous franchises in the history of the National Football League, had a reputation to defend — "Monsters of the Midway."

The fans stayed to watch the Bears' entertaining cast of characters: Walter Payton, football's all-time leading rusher; Jim McMahon, with his punk-rock style haircut and messages inscribed on his headbands; Richard Dent, the nimble defensive end who had hinted he might stay away from the game because he was unhappy with his contract; and Willie Gault, a world-class sprinter and wide receiver, who had brought his own acupuncturist from Tokyo to stick tiny needles into his body in an attempt to heal his aching back.

Who knows? Perhaps Super Bowl XXI will be more competitive. That one will be played on January 25, 1987, in the Rose Bowl in Pasadena, California.

The planning of the Super Bowl takes place years in advance, and the game seems to overshadow every other event. In 1985 Super Bowl XIX was scheduled for Stanford University in Palo Alto, California, on January 20. That was also the day Ronald Reagan was to be sworn in for his second term as President. Because people were worried that the Super Bowl and the Inauguration would compete with each other, many of the Inauguration parties were moved to Monday. Nobody wants to tangle with the Super Bowl.

In a time of diminishing revenue from television sports, Super Bowl XX earned approximately $32 million — before expenses — for the National Broadcasting Company. Commercials cost between $150,000 and $300,000 for half a minute. That is a huge expenditure, but it pays off because of the multimillion-plus audience.

The Super Bowl audience is increasing around the world. Rino Tommasi, the popular commentator on Italy's Canale Cinque (Channel Five) was present in New Orleans, telling his friends, "We will tape this and show it in my country tomorrow as *Monday Night Football.*" Italy also has its own football league, and it holds a championship every July.

The name of the game? Super Bowl. It has become a happening, an event, a television extravaganza, an excuse for a party.

Sometimes it is impossible to avoid attending a meeting, a classical-music concert, or a family wedding or birthday party on Super Bowl Sunday. But chances are that some fans will slip out to their car radios, or the nearest telephone, or a television set in the back room to find out the latest score in the big game.

The Super Bowl captures the attention of millions of people, but nobody is more involved than the 50 players on each team and their coaches. John Riggins, a proud and independent running back who once quit football for a year so he could live out on the plains in his beloved Kansas, returned to the game and led the Washington Redskins to the 1983 Super Bowl. As he and his linemen, the illustrious Hogs, prepared to meet the Miami Dolphins in Super Bowl XVII, Riggins shared a few of his thoughts:

"What does the Super Bowl mean? It's an opportunity to fulfill a dream. Other than that, it's just another football game. But the atmosphere is so extraordinary, it's not an ordinary work week."

Riggins was describing the excitement and the pageantry of a tradition only 20 years old. Some holidays take decades or even centuries to develop. The Super Bowl took only a few short years.

Life Before the Super Bowl

Once upon a time there was no Super Bowl.
It's hard to believe, but it's true. Once there were no 100-million-person television audiences, no late-January games, no flurry of colored balloons or white doves, no sky divers, no telephone calls from the President. How did the nation survive?

Survive it did, with a grand tradition of college football dating back to the 1800s. There was a spurt of professional football early in this century, but the real growth came immediately after World War I, when the National Football League was formed with franchises like the Green Bay Packers and the Decatur Staleys, later known as the Chicago Bears.

Pro football boasted heroes like Jim Thorpe, George Halas, Red Grange, and Bronco Nagurski in the 1930s. The old league officials did not regard the NFL as a form of show business, the way today's officials do. In the pre-television era, they did not feel the need to provide "entertainment." They had a sport, and that was entertaining enough.

The NFL produced memorable pre-Super Bowl title games like the one in 1940, when the Chicago

Bears, with Sid Luckman at quarterback, defeated the Washington Redskins, with Sammy Baugh at quarterback, by a lopsided 73–0 score.

After World War II, a rival league, the All-American Conference, produced a powerhouse franchise, the Cleveland Browns. When that league folded after the 1949 season, the Browns soon became a dominant team in the NFL.

Pro football entered the era of superlatives in 1958, when the Baltimore Colts beat the New York Giants, 23–17, in the first sudden-death overtime championship game in the league's history. The winning drive ended with a touchdown by Alan Ameche. The hard play of these two fine teams caused sports reporters and league officials to call it "The Greatest Football Game Ever Played."

With extensive coverage from television, helped by modern camera techniques, football soon competed with baseball as America's most popular team sport. Football was so popular that another rival league was formed late in 1959, leading directly to the Roman-numeral extravaganza known as the Super Bowl.

The new challenger was the American Football League, and it began to play in 1960 with franchises in Houston, Los Angeles, Dallas, Denver, Oakland, New York, Boston, and Buffalo. Soon the Dallas franchise moved to Kansas City and the Los Angeles franchise moved to San Diego.

The new league forced the new NFL commissioner, Pete Rozelle, to extend a Minnesota Vikings franchise to the Twin Cities of Minneapolis-St. Paul. The new league also put pressure on the old league with controversial two-point options for running or passing on extra points, creating last-minute 38–37 victories.

The new league liked to throw the ball a lot and display gaudy uniforms, but its most explosive weapon never flung a touchdown pass or ran for a two-point conversion. The American Football League's most potent asset was named Al Davis—and he was dynamite.

Al Davis was a shrewd football man from the decidedly nonfootball powerhouse of Brooklyn. He had worked his way up the ladder as an assistant coach until he landed in Oakland, where he became head coach, general manager, chief espionage agent, and one-man recruiting force for the Oakland Raiders.

The National Football League had always tried to appear to take the high road about recruiting players. Its teams drafted only college players who had graduated from college and become eligible for the draft. The NFL also did not believe in expensive bidding wars to hire new players.

The new league was more desperate. In 1963, the New York franchise changed its name from the Titans to the Jets. It also changed its stadium from the decrepit Polo Grounds to the new Shea Stadium. And its ownership changed from Harry Wismer to Sonny Werblin, a show-business executive with an eye for stars.

In 1965, Werblin outbid the St. Louis Cardinals for the services of Joe Willie Namath, a quarterback from the University of Alabama. Werblin paid the brash young man $427,000 a year, the highest salary in the history of the sport at the time. People were aghast at the high salary, but soon both leagues were paying even more for college players—and even waving money at players in the opposite leagues.

Al Davis believed in getting the best players, even if he and his assistants had to hide players in hotel rooms and offer them money and other inducements until they agreed to join the AFL. When the New York Giants of the NFL fired a salvo by signing Pete Gogolak, a placekicker from the Buffalo Bills of the AFL, the younger league got serious. On April 8, 1966, Al Davis was named commissioner of the AFL, and he went out and signed enough players from NFL clubs to make the NFL owners very nervous. *Very* nervous.

On June 8, 1966, the two leagues agreed to merge in time for the 1970 season. Al Davis resigned as AFL commissioner and promptly rejoined his old team, the Oakland Raiders, and Pete Rozelle remained commissioner of the NFL.

The two leagues agreed to play a championship game starting in 1967, but they did not refer to it as the Super Bowl. That came later.

SUPER BOWL I

Green Bay Packers 35—
Kansas City Chiefs 10
January 15, 1967, at Los Angeles

Super Ball,
Super Bowl

The first Super Bowl was played on January 15, 1967, but nobody knew it. People just called it the National Football League-American Football League World Championship Game. It was not a very catchy name.

Later it became known as the Super Bowl, partially because of two young children, Lamar Hunt, Jr., and Sharron Hunt, who were ten and eight years old, respectively, when the first Super Bowl was played.

Lamar Hunt was the owner of the old Dallas Texans in the AFL, but later he moved them to Kansas City and renamed them the Chiefs. In the 1966 season, the Chiefs beat Buffalo for the AFL title and qualified to play the Green Bay Packers, who had beaten Dallas in the NFL finals. The championship game was to be played in the Los Angeles Coliseum.

According to legend, one night during the season, Lamar Hunt had come home and nearly was knocked down by a giant ball bouncing around the house. His children told him it was called a "Super Ball."

Now he was on the committee to plan the new game. In a meeting one day, he tried to distinguish it from the other postseason games, and his words flowed something like this: "No, not those games — the one I mean is the final game — you know, the Super Bowl."

He said he had not planned to called it the Super Bowl but that the name just popped into his head because of his children's toy. Years later he wrote: "The response was less than overwhelming. I think we were really more interested in when the room-service lunch would come." But shortly afterward, committee members began to refer to it casually as the Super Bowl.

The public did not think about it until Roman numerals were applied several years later, but the name began with two children playing with a ball. A round ball, incidentally. Not a football.

The Chiefs did not do so well with a football. The Packers, one of the oldest franchises in pro football, had been rebuilt by Vince Lombardi, a gruff New Yorker with, according to his players, a heart of gold. The Packers had won NFL titles in 1961, 1962, 1965, and 1966.

The Packers were not a subtle team. In their green-and-gold uniforms, they employed simple running and passing plays, featuring hard blocking, and their defense was also basic and physical. The Packers did well because their games seemed like a vacation after Vince Lombardi's practices.

"Coach Lombardi treats us all the same," quipped one of the Packers. "Like dogs."

The Packers had all-league players like Bart Starr at quarterback, Jim Taylor at fullback, Ray Nitschke at linebacker, Herb Adderley at cornerback, and Forrest Gregg at tackle. They did not need Vince Lombardi's blunt locker-room talks to know they were representing not only themselves and the tiny city of Green Bay, Wisconsin, but also the established NFL. They did not want to lose to upstarts.

"A loss here would ruin all that Coach Lombardi has built up over the years," said Packer defensive back Tom Brown. "That thought haunts us and drives us."

The upstarts from Kansas City were a typical and successful AFL team, using fancy plays from the notebook of coach Hank Stram, a dapper and talkative man who later became a television broadcaster. The Chiefs had an all-star line, a passing combination of Len Dawson to Otis Taylor, and a talkative cornerback named Fred Williamson — now an actor.

Williamson called himself "The Hammer" and bragged of his karate-chop tackles that had broken, he claimed, 30 helmets. He made good copy for reporters. The Packers saved the articles.

Only 61,946 fans showed up for the first interleague championship. The AFL fans cheered when Kansas City stopped Green Bay's first drive. They didn't mind when Boyd Dowler, the Green Bay flanker, hurt his shoulder on the sixth play.

Dowler's replacement was Max McGee, a 34-year-old veteran who later admitted he had partied until six A.M., never dreaming he would have to play much on Sunday. As the game began, McGee was resting in the shade on the Packer bench, perhaps dreaming of the $15,000 check all the Packers would receive for the game. Suddenly he heard Lombardi bark, "McGee!"

Now McGee had to work in the warm midday sun of Los Angeles. Starting on the Kansas City 37-yard line, he cut inside Willie Mitchell, a young cornerback the Packers had decided to exploit.

Starr's pass was a little weak, and McGee, while running at full speed, had to reach behind with his right hand to make the difficult catch.

"When the ball stuck in it, I almost fainted," he said years later.

He held the ball, tucked it in his left arm, and chugged into the end zone with the first touchdown in Super Bowl history.

Kansas City came back to tie the score on a touchdown pass from Dawson to fullback Curt McClinton, but Jim Taylor scored on a 14-yard run to make it 14–7 Green Bay. Mike Mercer kicked a 31-yard field goal for the Chiefs to cut the deficit to 14–10.

At the half, Lombardi delivered one of his typical blistering speeches, reminding the Packers they were only four points ahead of an AFL team, for goodness' sakes.

"He was right," said Fred (Fuzzy) Thurston, a veteran guard. "I don't want some guy coming into my steak house [in Green Bay] and saying, 'You played on the first team to lose to the AFL.'"

In the second half, the Packers dominated. Three charging Packers forced a 40-yard interception by Willie Wood, which was followed by a five-yard scoring run by Elijah Pitts. Later, the wily McGee victimized young Mitchell again for a 13-yard touchdown. In the fourth period, the Packers scored on a one-yard run by Pitts.

The Packers also had the satisfaction of seeing Donny Anderson run down Fred Williamson in the fourth quarter. The Hammer was knocked unconscious and did not play again that day.

"We were through, and we knew it," Williamson said later.

McGee caught seven passes for 138 yards and two touchdowns — not a bad output for a man who had not expected to play. Starr completed 16 of 23 passes for 250 yards and was chosen the game's Most Valuable Player. The Packers praised the Chiefs but added they did not think the Chiefs could match the NFL's top teams.

The NFL had saved its pride and sense of separation — for a little while longer, anyway.

SUPER BOWL II

**Green Bay Packers 33 —
Oakland Raiders 14
January 14, 1968, at Miami**

The Pack Was Back

This time Al Davis's Raiders got a chance to test the mighty Packers. Davis, who had thrown fear into the established NFL by his raiding tactics before the merger, hoped to even the score for the AFL before it lost its separate identity in the 1970 season.

The Raiders, in their silver-and-black uniforms — in later years compared to the fearsome Darth Vader of *Star Wars* — roared through the 1967 season with 13 victories and only one loss, and in the AFL title game they crushed Houston, 40–7.

The Packers had a tough time in the NFL's feared "frostbite" division, winning nine but losing four and tying one. However, they roared past Los Angeles and nipped Dallas in the NFL championship game.

The second Super Bowl was played in Miami, Florida. There were hints that Vince Lombardi would retire after this game, and his players vowed to win this game for their coach.

The Raiders were a rough bunch in their own league, with a huge defensive end, Ben Davidson, best known for breaking the cheekbone of glamorous New York Jet quarterback Joe Namath. Davidson rode a motorcycle and sported a handlebar mustache that heightened the Hell's Angels image he enjoyed.

The Raiders learned their lesson from the mishaps of Fred (the Hammer) Williamson the year before. They did not brag about what they would do to the Packers. Instead, they talked respectfully of the Packers. It turned out they were right.

Like any good sports organization, the Packers had carefully rearranged their roster after a championship season, not letting sentiment keep favorite players in uniform too long. Jim Taylor had been allowed to join a new team, the New Orleans Saints, in his native Louisiana. Paul Hornung, once the premier halfback of pro football, had retired. And several other Packers had been phased out through injuries. But the Packers had replaced them with young, speedy players like Travis Williams, who set a league record by returning four kickoffs for touchdowns.

There were 75,546 fans in the Orange Bowl on January 14, 1968, as Bart Starr began picking apart the Raiders just as he had done to the Chiefs in the Super Bowl before. His short, crisp passes set up two field goals by Don Chandler early in the game.

Then, as the Raider cornerbacks began edging closer to the line of scrimmage, Starr sent Boyd Dowler deep down the middle for a surprise 62-yard touchdown play.

Oakland came back and moved 78 yards in nine plays as Daryle Lamonica threw a 23-yard scoring pass to Bill Miller. The Raiders then stopped the Packers, but Roger Bird fumbled a punt and it was recovered by a Green Bay rookie, Dick Capp. Chandler kicked a 43-yard field goal for a 16–7 halftime lead.

In the second half, Starr threw a surprise 35-yard pass to Max McGee on a short-yardage play, setting up Don Anderson's 2-yard touchdown run. Chandler added a fourth field goal, and all-pro defender Herb Adderley scored a 60-yard interception before Lamonica threw another 23-yard touchdown pass to Miller.

The final score was Green Bay 33, Oakland 14.

Once again, Starr was chosen the Most Valuable Player, but Ray Nitschke, the balding linebacker with gaps where his teeth used to be, was also praised for making five unassisted tackles, four assists on tackles, and plenty of intimidation. Also, Don Chandler's total of 15 points, on four field goals and three extra points, became a Super Bowl record that still exists, going into the 1984 game. (Lombardi did retire after the game. He later coached the Washington Redskins before he died in 1970.)

The Raiders packed their grim uniforms and looked forward to being the first AFL team to win a Super Bowl in the following year. It was Al Davis's great dream, but he was not to achieve that honor.

SUPER BOWL III

**New York Jets 16—
Baltimore Colts 7
January 12, 1969, at Miami**

The Jets Make History

The honor of being the first AFL team to win
the Super Bowl went to one of Al Davis's
biggest rivals, the New York Jets. In only the third
Super Bowl, the Jets were to strike a great blow
for their league, years before most people expected
an AFL victory.

Just to be in the Super Bowl was a major ac-
complishment for the Jets, who had begun as the
unstable team called the New York Titans, playing
in the ramshackle old Polo Grounds. But a show-
business impresario, Sonny Werblin, changed their
name and their image in new Shea Stadium, by
providing Joe Namath, the brash quarterback from
Alabama.

In the 1968 season, the $427,000 quarterback
led the Jets to a 11–3 record and then a 27–23
victory over Oakland — a score that Al Davis, to
this day, regards as one of his most bitter defeats.

The Jets were obviously a good team, coached by roly-poly Weeb Ewbank, who had coached the Colts in earlier days. They had two good running backs, Emerson Boozer and Matt Snell; two excellent receivers in Don Maynard and George Sauer, Jr.; and fine defensive linemen like Gerry Philbin and Verlon Biggs.

But the gamblers and the sports reporters felt the Jets deserved being 18-point underdogs to the NFL champions, the Baltimore Colts. Baltimore had compiled a 13–1 record during the season and had then beaten Minnesota and Cleveland in play-off games.

The Colts were coached by Don Shula, a rugged-looking former defensive back who looked trim enough to step into the Colts' backfield. He was also tough enough to have benched the former all-pro quarterback with a sore elbow, Johnny Unitas, in favor of Earl Morrall.

The Colts had dependable runners and receivers and smart, tough defenders. In theory, they had all the advantages. But they didn't have Joe Namath.

Namath had gained his nickname "Broadway Joe" from his glamorous bachelor life in Manhattan. He was brash and he was good, with an arm that could fire a football 50 yards or more. And he was pretty good at slinging words, too.

Super Bowl III was to be held in the Orange

Bowl in Miami on January 12, 1969. By this time, the two leagues were getting used to promoting the big game. They staged a Photo Day on Monday for the benefit of the hundreds of news photographers sent to the game.

Joe Namath did not show up for Photo Day. Ten A.M. was too early for him. But he was not shy about appearing in public after dark. Lou Michaels, the rugged 32-year-old placekicker for the Colts, spotted Namath in a restaurant one night. Lou was the brother of Walt Michaels, an assistant coach with the Jets.

"You're doing a lot of talking," Lou Michaels said.

"There's a lot to talk about," Namath said. "We're going to kick hell out of your team."

"Haven't you heard of the word modesty, Joseph?" Michaels asked.

The two men seemed on the verge of fisticuffs, but they quickly became friends and left the restaurant, laughing, an hour later. However, the rumors got around Florida that Michaels and Namath had nearly come to blows.

"Aw, he's all right," Michaels said.

Just in case anybody missed Namath's aspirations, Joe made them public at the Touchdown Club banquet on the Thursday before the game.

"The Jets will win. I guarantee it," Namath told the audience.

The Colts did not take kindly to Namath's words; they hoped to do something about it on Sunday and also maintain the NFL's superiority in the Super Bowl.

The Jets' determination was obvious to the 75,377 fans the first time the Jets had the ball that Sunday. Snell, fuming over being compared unfavorably to the Baltimore runners, ran so hard on a 7-yard gain that he knocked out Rick Volk, the Colt safety.

The Jets didn't score on that drive, but Baltimore showed its vulnerability when Lou Michaels missed an attempted field goal. Later, Al Atkinson, a Jet linebacker, tipped an apparent touchdown pass by Morrall into an interception for the Jets' Randy Beverly.

The Jets continued to make things happen their way, driving 80 yards to score, with Snell rushing for the touchdown from the 4-yard line.

Tom Matte aroused Baltimore's hopes with a 58-yard run — still the longest run from scrimmage in Super Bowl history — but then Morrall was intercepted by Johnny Sample, a volatile cornerback who had once played for Ewbank with the Colts.

Late in the half, Morrall didn't spot open receiver Jimmy Orr and threw an interception instead. The Jets' Jim Turner kicked two field goals for a 13–0 halftime lead.

With the Jets' defense stopping Morrall, Namath

played conservatively, moving the Jets on time-consuming running plays until Turner kicked his third field goal for a 16–0 lead.

Shula sent in Unitas, in his familiar No. 19 and his old-fashioned ankle-length shoes, and the future Hall-of-Fame quarterback sparked a touchdown drive with 3:19 left. But it was too late to salvage victory or pride. The final score was 16–7.

Weeb Ewbank, the chubby coach who had led the Baltimore Colts to their famous 23–17 victory over the New York Giants in the NFL title game of 1958, now savored his latest championship.

"They called that one 'The Greatest Game,'" Ewbank said. "But I'll take this one."

So would his players. So would the New York fans. And so would everybody in the American Football League. The AFL had its first Super Bowl champion, and it took only three tries.

SUPER BOWL IV

Kansas City Chiefs 23 —
Minnesota Vikings 7
January 11, 1970, at New Orleans

The Chiefs Return

The old riverfront city of New Orleans was
bustling in early January of 1970. Two rival
groups crowded the narrow streets of the Old
Quarter, chanting and cheering for opposing football teams. For a time, it appeared that the best
blocking and tackling might be conducted by Minnesota Viking and Kansas City Chief fans right
out on Bourbon, Canal, and Rampart streets.

The occasion was Super Bowl IV, to be held in
the intimate and exotic city of New Orleans. This
was to be the last "pure" meeting between the
NFL and AFL champions because interlocking
schedules were to begin in the 1970 regular season.
It was the first time the Super Bowl had a one-
week preparation period instead of two, which
would not happen again until the strike-plagued
season of 1982–83.

One team was familiar to the Super Bowl. Many
of the Chiefs remembered losing to Green Bay in

the 1967 game and wanted to make up for it. The Chiefs had come a long way in the 1969 season, finishing behind Oakland during the Western Division race but then beating the defending champions, the Jets, in a play-off and beating Oakland, 17–7, in the AFL title game.

The Chiefs were convinced their time had come. Snazzy coach Hank Stram had polished up his multiple-offense attack, labeling it "the new football."

Stram said: "The trend of the 1960s was basic simplicity, the way of the Packers and now the Vikings. The trend of the 1970s will go more to a varied game like ours. You might say this game is a meeting between the old and the new."

Stram thought it was significant that this meeting took place on only the second Sunday of a new decade (1970). But more significant was Stram's imaginative passing attack, carried out by Len Dawson, with passes to Frank Pitts and Otis Taylor and running by little Mike Garrett.

The Chiefs had the same good offensive line as in Super Bowl I and had brought in new defensive stars like tackle Curley Culp, linebacker Willie Lanier, and cornerbacks Emmitt Thomas and Jim Marsalis.

The Vikings played some defense themselves. Their front line of Carl Eller, Alan Page, Gary Larsen, and Jim Marshall was known as "the Purple People Eaters." They were not big, but they were quick and resourceful. The Vikings were a tough team, led by a lean outdoorsman, Bud Grant, who was more comfortable in a duck blind than in a living room and did not allow his players to wear gloves or warm themselves on sideline heaters in the wintry blasts at Metropolitan Stadium.

That was fine with Joe Kapp, a brawling, inspirational quarterback whose slogan "forty for sixty" (40 players, 60 minutes) had sparked the team. His passes fluttered, but his head-on crash into Cleveland's linebacker, Jim Houston, had been a highlight of the NFL title game.

New Orleans was chilly and rainy on Sunday as the largest crowd of the four Super Bowls — 80,562 fans — jammed into Tulane Stadium.

Dawson had been agitated during the week when his name surfaced in a probe of gambling activities, but authorities had insisted he was under no suspicion.

"Everything was on the line," he would say years later after becoming a television broadcaster. "I felt we had to win or it would be hanging over my head for the rest of my life."

Needing to be nearly perfect to avoid any unfair comments, Dawson moved Kansas City to within range for three field goals by Norwegian-born Jan Stenerud; Jan kicked with the side of his foot, soccer-style.

Late in the half, Minnesota's Charlie West fumbled a kickoff, and Remi Prudhamme recovered for Kansas City on the Vikings' 19-yard line. Six plays later, Garrett started running to his right, but cut back over left guard for the 5-yard touchdown that gave the Chiefs a 16–0 halftime lead.

Joe Kapp was no quitter, and he came out after halftime and engineered a 69-yard scoring drive that ended with Dave Osborn's 3-yard touchdown. But Dawson came right back with a scoring drive that ended with a 46-yard scoring pass to Otis Taylor, who sidestepped Earsell Mackbee on his way to the end zone.

Early in the fourth period, Aaron Brown of Kansas City put Kapp out of the game with a hard tackle. The Chiefs limited the Vikings to only 67 yards in rushing and won the game, 23–7. The victory evened the score with two Super Bowls each for the NFL and AFL, and put the underdog Chiefs on top of football as the 1970s began.

"But the best thing about today's game," said Len Dawson, who was chosen the Most Valuable Player, "is that we don't have to answer for it the next three years, as we did after our last Super Bowl. This time we're the champions."

SUPER BOWL V

Baltimore Colts 16 —
Dallas Cowboys 13
January 17, 1971, at Miami

Mother Knows Best

On the night before Super Bowl V, Jim O'Brien made a telephone call to his mother, who occasionally told fortunes based on the positions of the stars.

O'Brien had an intense interest in the Super Bowl, since he was a rookie placekicker with the Baltimore Colts, who were about to meet the Dallas Cowboys in the Orange Bowl on January 17, 1971.

"She said we'd win it by a close margin," O'Brien said later. "She's an astrologer and she's told me a lot of other things that turned out right."

O'Brien had other reasons to suspect a close Super Bowl, after four straight one-sided games. He had had a dream in which somebody kicked a field goal to decide the game.

"The dream wasn't in Technicolor," O'Brien reported later. "I couldn't tell what team it was."

Even his teammates had an inkling it would be a close game. During practices that week, they had screamed insults at him, like "You'll never make it" and "You just don't have it" whenever he attempted a kick in practice. This was, of course, to toughen him up. They suspected the opposing players and fans might try to rattle a rookie about to make the kick of his life.

O'Brien was one of the few young players on the Colts, who had smarted following their loss to the Jets in the third Super Bowl. But now it was two years later, and the Super Bowl had officially been given its Roman numeral V, making the first four games I, II, III, and IV in retrospect.

The curious thing about the first Super Bowl following the full merger of the NFL and AFL was that it matched two NFL teams. The Colts, along with Pittsburgh and Cleveland, had agreed to move into the new American Conference to balance the two conferences at 13 teams each. Baltimore then beat Cincinnati, a young franchise, and Oakland, to gain the Super Bowl.

The Colts had a new coach, Don McCafferty, following Don Shula's move to Miami. McCafferty had returned 37-year-old Johnny Unitas to quarterback once his elbow had healed, putting Earl Morral in reserve again.

The Cowboys had never won an NFL championship under coach Tom Landry, but football people knew Dallas was one of the best organizations in the league, with excellent coaching and scouting. The only question was whether analytical, unemotional Tom Landry could ever win the final game on an emotional Super Sunday.

The Cowboys had a fine running attack built around Duane Thomas, Calvin Hill, Walt Garrison, and Dan Reeves. Their passing attack featured Craig Morton throwing to Bob Hayes, once an Olympic sprinter.

Dallas's defense bothered Unitas early in the game, as Chuck Howley, a linebacker, made a diving interception after bobbling the ball. Both teams traded mistakes until Mike Clark kicked a field goal for Dallas—not what Jim O'Brien's mother had dreamed. After penalties cost Dallas a possible touchdown, Clark kicked another field goal for a 6–0 lead.

Unitas's aging arm overthrew a pass, but it worked to the Colts' advantage as Eddie Hinton barely got his fingers on the ball. The ball popped into the air and tipped the fingertips of Dallas's Mel Renfro before John Mackey, Baltimore's superb tight end, grabbed it for a 75-yard touchdown play. The Cowboys argued vehemently that Renfro never touched the ball and that Mackey had caught it illegally, but the officials would not bend. In another bad omen for Jim O'Brien's predictions, Dallas blocked the extra point, keeping the score tied at 6–6.

"After the kick was blocked, I thought I was going to fold," O'Brien said years later. "I mean, I didn't think I'd be any good for the rest of the game."

A fumble by Unitas set up a 7-yard touchdown to silent Duane Thomas, giving Dallas a 13–6 lead at the half.

Late in the first half, Unitas suffered a fractured rib when he was tackled by 250-pound Georgie Andrie. This gave Morrall a chance to redeem his 1969 loss to the Jets.

Morrall moved the Colts to the Dallas 2-yard line, where the Cowboys stopped Norm Bulaich three straight times. Rather than let O'Brien try for an almost automatic field goal, the new coach, McCafferty, called for a pass from Morrall to Tom Mitchell, which failed. McCafferty knew he would be blamed if the spurned field goal cost the Colts the game.

In the second half, both teams continued to make crucial mistakes. Baltimore's Jerry Logan forced Thomas to fumble near the goal line, costing Dallas a touchdown. But Morton was intercepted by Rick Volk, who had been badly hurt in Super Bowl III two years earlier. Volk's steal set up a 2-yard touchdown by Tom Nowatzke with 6:53 left, and O'Brien's extra point tied the score.

With 59 seconds left, Baltimore's Mike Curtis intercepted a Morton pass and ran it from the Cowboys' 41 to the 28. The Colts gained only three yards in two plays as the clock ticked down to nine seconds remaining.

The Colts sent O'Brien on the field, and just as expected, the Cowboys tried to rattle him by calling time, to give him extra time to worry.

O'Brien said years later: "I hoped it wouldn't come down to me to win it. Who needs that kind of pressure? The money's just as good if somebody else wins it for you."

But O'Brien was going to have to try to win the money for his older teammates. McCafferty ordered Morrall to talk to O'Brien to calm him down, but Morrall didn't need to be told.

"Obie, we got plenty of time," Morrall said.

Just as predicted, players and fans did yell "choke" at O'Brien as the rookie prepared to kick. But just as predicted, O'Brien kicked a 32-yard field goal with five seconds remaining for a 16–13 Baltimore victory. The humiliating loss to the Jets could now be put in the past. Now Dallas was the team with an incentive to come back and win a Super Bowl on the second try.

SUPER BOWL VI

Dallas Cowboys 24—Miami Dolphins 3
January 16, 1972, at New Orleans

The Cowboys Arrive

When the Dallas Cowboys reached their first Super Bowl in 1971, reporters asked Duane Thomas, a rookie running back, if he was nervous.

"No," replied Thomas, a man of few words.

But, somebody said, this is the big game, the ultimate game.

"If it's the ultimate game, how come they're playing another one next year?" Thomas demanded in a speech that was exceptionally long for him.

He had a point. One day short of a year later, in Tulane Stadium in New Orleans, another Super Bowl was held. And the Dallas Cowboys were back for another try.

The Cowboy organization, one of the most efficient in pro football, had suffered all year with the same old tag that the Cowboys could not win the big game. Coach Tom Landry and the front office knew they had the right components for a championship, but they decided to make one vital change during the 1971 season.

Instead of using Craig Morton as the regular quarterback, the Cowboys switched to Roger Staubach, once an all-American at the U.S. Naval Academy. Few people had believed that Staubach could spend his mandatory five years in the Navy after college and then qualify as a professional quarterback, but Staubach was one of a kind.

"Other quarterbacks lay down before you can hit them," a rival coach said. "This Staubach guy thinks he's a running back."

The Cowboys had other running backs, notably Duane Thomas, who rarely talked to teammates or coaches or the press, but who could carry the ball in traffic.

The Dolphins were coached by Don Shula, who had coached Baltimore in its Super Bowl III loss to the Jets. The Dolphins were an emerging football team, with runners like Larry Csonka and Jim Kiick, a quarterback named Bob Griese, a superior receiver in Paul Warfield, and a defense that was proud of calling itself "the No-Name Defense."

To qualify for the Super Bowl, the Dolphins had first beaten Kansas City, 27–24, in overtime on a 37-yard field goal by Garo Yepremian. The game had taken 82 minutes and 40 seconds and was the longest game in football history. In the AFC final, they beat Baltimore, 21–0. The Cowboys had beaten Minnesota and San Francisco.

Super Bowl VI began with Chuck Howley —

the Most Valuable Player in defeat in Super Bowl V — recovering Csonka's first fumble of the year.

The Cowboys ran two lineman at Nick Buoniconti, Miami's small but excellent linebacker, in a drive that ended in a Mike Clark field goal.

Soon Bob Lilly, the Cowboys' fine tackle, chased Griese for a massive 29-yard loss, putting the Dolphins in poor field position. This later enabled Staubach to run off a scoring drive that ended with a 7-yard touchdown pass to Lance Alworth.

Miami scored a field goal by Yepremian late in the first half, but Thomas and Walt Garrison blasted through Miami's defenses time and time again in the third period. In a 71-yard drive, Staubach threw only one pass before Thomas ran for a 3-yard touchdown.

A 41-yard run with an interception by Howley in the fourth period set up a 9-yard scoring pass from Staubach to Mike Ditka that ended the scoring, with the Cowboys winning, 24–3.

Even Duane Thomas managed a word for the television audience. A nervous announcer stuck a microphone in front of the stone-faced running back and made a comment that Thomas had seemed "quick and fast."

"Evidently," Thomas said.

That was enough. He had done all his talking with 95 yards gained and a touchdown. Staubach had been voted the Most Valuable Player, and the Dallas Cowboys had answered all their critics.

"The load is off our shoulders; we won the big one," Bob Lilly shouted.

Duane Thomas couldn't have said it better.

SUPER BOWL VII

**Miami Dolphins 14—
Washington Redskins 7
January 14, 1973, at Los Angeles**

Miami's Quest for Perfection

Can a football team play a perfect season? Some people would argue that the Miami Dolphins had a perfect season that began in 1972 and ended in the Los Angeles Memorial Coliseum on January 14, 1973, in Super Bowl VII.

The Dolphins bounced back from their loss to the Cowboys in Super Bowl VI to win all 14 regular-season games in 1972. They scored 385 points, the most in the league, and they gave up only 171 points, the fewest in the league.

In the play-offs, they beat Cleveland by six points and up-and-coming Pittsburgh by four points. Then they roared into the Super Bowl and beat the Washington Redskins, 14–7.

But their season was not perfect.

Near the end of the Super bowl, Garó Yepremian, the Dolphins' placekicker, committed a play that people were talking about a decade later. It was a combination blocked field goal-attempted pass-fumble that brought a much needed sense of humor to the often ponderous Super Bowl atmosphere.

Yepremian's famous play took place with about seven minutes left in the game and the Dolphins trying to improve on their 14–0 lead.

Washington, one of pro football's more venerable franchises, had advanced to their first Super Bowl by winning 11 of 14 games during the season and beating first Green Bay and then Dallas in the National Conference play-offs.

The Redskins were coached by George Allen, a smooth-talking Californian whose entire life was spent thinking of football. His wife had once explained that Allen ate mostly ice cream because "he doesn't have to chew it. You have to concentrate when you chew food. And that would take his mind away from football."

Allen had accumulated experienced players by trading away most of his college draft choices in the near future. His quarterbacks were the ancient Sonny Jurgensen and Bill Kilmer, his linemen were not exactly young either, and the Redskin team was nicknamed "The Over the Hill Gang." It was also a rough, smart, and capable group of men who enjoyed playing for Allen.

But in Super Bowl VII, the Redskins were up against near perfection. They crossed midfield only once in the first half as Miami exploited their defenses.

The third time Miami had the ball, it moved 63 yards to score. A key play was an 18-yard pass from Bob Griese to Paul Warfield, and the touchdown pass was a 28-yard play from Griese to Howard Twilley.

The extra point was kicked by Garo Yepremian. (A native of the island of Cyprus, he had come to the U.S. as a soccer player and earned a job with the Dolphins, kicking a football with the side of his foot. He was nearly bald, quite small, spoke English, Armenian, Turkish, and Greek, and sold designer ties in his spare time.)

Washington made a mild threat late in the first half, moving to the Miami 48-yard line. But Nick Buoniconti, the small linebacking star of the No-Name Defense, intercepted Kilmer and returned the ball 32 yards to the Washington 27-yard line.

Jim Kiick ran for three yards; his partner, Larry Csonka, ran for three, Griese passed to Jim Mandich for 19 yards, and Kiick ran other yard. With 18 seconds left in the half, Kiick ran for the touchdown. Yepremian added the extra point.

Excellent defensive work by the Dolphins' Jake Scott, the game's Most Valuable Player, helped keep the score at 14–0 late in the game. Many of the 90,182 fans were becoming restive.

"The game was very boring and I felt bad for the networks," Yepremian would joke a decade later. "People were turning off their TV sets and I had to do something to liven things up."

With 2:07 remaining, the Dolphins tried a 42-yard field goal, but the snap from center Howard Kindig was low, and quarterback Earl Morrall, formerly with Baltimore, hurriedly tried to set it up for Yepremian.

However, the desperate Over the Hill Gang swarmed in, and tackle Bill Brundige blocked the kick. The ball bounced back toward Yepremian, who, at 5 feet 7 inches, didn't really want to be smothered.

For the first time in his life, Yepremian cranked up his arm to throw a pass. The ball slipped out of his tiny fingers, and he tried to bat it toward a teammate. However, Mike Bass, the Redskins' defensive back, scooped it away from him and ran 49 yards for one of the ugliest touchdowns in history.

On the sidelines, Don Shula, still looking for his first Super Bowl victory after two losses, looked grim enough to tackle Yepremian. However, the Dolphins had not won 16 straight games by accident. Norm Evans, Miami's tackle, said in the huddle: "We all know what we have to do now. So let's just do it."

They gave the ball to Kiick and Csonka and killed enough time so that Washington had only a fleeting chance to score and didn't. The perfect season — well, nearly perfect — was over, with a score of 14–7.

"This is the greatest moment of my whole coaching career," Shula said in the happy dressing room.

Some of the Dolphins were so angry with Yepremian for letting Bass get the ball that they did not speak to him for months. But during the off-season, Shula wrote a letter thanking Yepremian for a good season—and firmly requesting that he refrain from throwing any passes in the following season.

Miami Dolphins 24 —
Minnesota Vikings 7
January 13, 1974, at Houston

New Site, Old Teams

The Super Bowl moved to a new site in 1974, the Rice University Stadium in Houston, Texas. Although the site was new, the teams were not. For the first time in the eight years of the Super Bowl, both teams had played in the championship game before.

The Miami Dolphins, losers of Super Bowl VI and winners of Super Bowl VII, were back. So were the Minnesota Vikings, who had lost in the chill and rain of New Orleans back in Super Bowl IV.

The Vikings were eager to win their first Super Bowl. Their rugged quarterback of 1970, Joe Kapp, was no longer playing. Instead of a quarterback who liked to run over people, the Vikings now had a quarterback who liked to run away from people: Francis Asbury Tarkenton.

Named for a famous Methodist missionary, Tarkenton had been the first hero of the Minnesota franchise in the early 1960s but had been traded away to the lowly New York Giants by the former coach, Norm van Brocklin.

Now Tarkenton had been brought "home" to play for Bud Grant, and he was running his familiar "scrambling" routes to escape tacklers. Kapp had once leveled a defensive man who got in his way. Tarkenton preferred to wear out the hulking defensive linemen by letting them chase him around the backfield for a while.

When a tackler approached, Tarkenton would slip out of bounds at the last possible moment or slide onto the ground like a baseball player stealing second base. Either way, he survived to scramble again.

With Tarkenton back home and the Purple People Eaters still chewing it up as a front defensive line, the Vikings had a 12–2 record in the 1973 season and then beat Washington and Dallas in the play-offs.

After its perfect 1972 season, capped with Garo Yepremian's famous blunder in the Super Bowl VII victory, the Dolphins had won 12 of 14 games in 1973. In the play-offs, the Dolphins had beaten Cincinnati and Oakland. They had pretty much the same cast as in the two previous Super Bowls, with Larry Csonka and Jim Kiick — sometimes nicknamed Butch Cassidy and the Sundance Kid — seeming tougher than ever.

Csonka had gained over 1,000 yards in each of the Dolphins' three straight Super Bowl years. He was a big, tough farm boy from Ohio who weighed 238 pounds and did not mind sticking all of it into the tacklers.

"It's nice to know that you're punishing those guys as much as they're punishing you," Csonka once said.

Even a star runner like Csonka is only as good as his offensive line, and most of the linemen were hurt in 1973. Larry Little had a bad knee, Wayne Moore had a bad knee and dislocated shoulder, Norm Evans had a bad ankle, Jim Langer had a bruised calf muscle, and Bob Kuechenberg had broken his arm a few weeks earlier.

Kuechenberg was used to hard times in football. He had been cut by two NFL teams and then had played for $200 a game with the Chicago Owls in a semipro league. He often told his Dolphin teammates about the Owls' grubby locker room, where, he said, they kept giant cats to kill the giant rats.

Kuechenberg was glad to have fought his way out of the semipro league to the Super Bowl champions. He was the kind of battler who would continue to fight on Super Bowl turf.

When the two teams met on January 13, 1974, the Dolphins' front line blasted holes in the Viking defense with a 62-yard drive in nine plays after the kickoff; Csonka scored from the 5-yard line.

The next time the Dolphins got the ball, they moved 56 yards with Kiick scoring from the 1. Garo Yepremian refrained from trying to throw the ball and kicked both extra points and added a 28-yard field goal for a 17–0 lead.

If the Vikings could get some points on the scoreboard, the game could still be close. Tarkenton moved his team just before halftime, advancing to the Dolphins' 8-yard line on second down. Oscar Reed gained only one yard in two carries. On fourth down, Reed seemingly bulled over for a first down, only to have Nick Buoniconti jar the ball loose.

Jake Scott recovered the ball to break up the challenge. The No-Name Defense was as tough as ever. In the third period, Bob Griese's pass to Paul Warfield set up Csonka's touchdown that made the score 24–0 and sent some of the fans scurrying for the exits to avoid the traffic jam.

Tarkenton finally slipped in for a touchdown in the final period, but the Dolphins won their second straight Super Bowl, 24–7. Up to that point, only Green Bay had won two straight Super Bowls.

In the closing minutes, two of the most intelligent and brave linemen, Kuechenberg of Miami and Alan Page of Minnesota, squared off, after Page had tackled Griese from behind, thinking the quarterback still had the ball. Kuechenberg went to the defense of Griese, but the two big linemen were separated before they could come to blows.

"You can understand why he felt the way he did. This is a big one to lose," Kuechenberg said later.

The Vikings had lost again, and now the Dolphins had two straight titles and Larry Csonka had set a record for the Super Bowl by carrying the ball 33 times for 145 yards. Csonka gave all the credit to his linemen, particularly Bob Kuechenberg, who had played with the fire that only a refugee from the Chicago Owls could muster.

SUPER BOWL IX

Pittsburgh Steelers 16 —
Minnesota Vikings 6
January 12, 1975, at New Orleans

The Steelers Reward "the Chief"

When Franco Harris reported to the Pittsburgh Steelers in 1972, some members of the team didn't think he would make it. He was not the most intense running back anybody had ever seen. And he didn't go out of his way to be a hit.

The tough steelworkers in Pittsburgh did not take kindly to his reflective, gliding, opt-for-the-sidelines style. But Franco Harris grew on people. He helped the Steelers reach the play-offs in his first two seasons, and in 1974 he led them to the Super Bowl.

The Steelers had been in the league 44 years by this time, owned by Arthur Rooney, a popular, cigar-smoking Pittsburgh man who suffered more than his own fans from the repeated failures of the Steelers.

In the early 1970s, Rooney and his sons and a new coach, Chuck Noll, built a contender with a quarterback named Terry Bradshaw, a defensive lineman known as Mean Joe Greene, and Franco Harris from Mount Holly, N.J.

In 1972, Harris brought the owner and the old city one of their greatest moments. In a play-off game against Oakland, Harris caught a pass that had been deflected by an Oakland defender, Jack Tatum, and ran 60 yards with a winning, last-minute touchdown. Rooney, who had already taken the elevator to the dressing room to congratulate Oakland, was told he had won the game. Harris's catch is still called "The Miraculous Reception" in Pittsburgh.

In 1974, the Steelers were eager for their first Super Bowl appearance. They won ten, lost three, and tied one before beating Buffalo and Oakland for the American Conference title.

Rooney had been such a good sport that he had given up some of his old NFL rivalries and moved into the American Conference to help balance the two conferences after the merger.

In 1974, Minnesota again dominated the National Conference, showing a 10–4 record and beating St. Louis and Los Angeles to qualify for the Super Bowl. Bud Grant's Vikings seemed as good as ever, with Fran Tarkenton at quarterback, the

Purple People Eaters up front on defense, and rugged Chuck Foreman lugging the ball.

The site of Super Bowl IX was Tulane Stadium, on January 12, 1975. The Vikings had lost their first Super Bowl attempt there five years earlier, as well as Super Bowl VIII in Texas. The Vikings, however seemed confident of winning on their third try.

The game was still scoreless midway through the second period as Tarkenton tried to lead the Vikings from deep in their own territory. The wily, scrambling quarterback called a fake pitchout and tried to hand off to fullback Dave Osborn. Instead, the ball hit another Viking and bounced toward the end zone.

Knowing that if the Steelers recovered the ball, it would be a touchdown, Tarkenton tried to grab the ball and keep it out of the end zone. He was half successful, regaining possession but sliding into the end zone.

The Steelers' Dwight White — who had spent much of the week in the hospital with a viral infection — tackled him for a two-point safety.

Pittsburgh still led, 2–0, when it kicked off the second half. Minnesota's Bill Brown fumbled and Marv Kellum recovered for the Steelers. Rocky Bleier, who had recovered from injuries suffered while in the army in Vietnam, carried the ball first for the Steelers. Then Franco took over.

As usual, Harris looked for the easiest route rather than the hardest. He found one down the left side, worth 24 yards. After a 3-yard loss, he turned the left corner for a 12-yard touchdown run and a 9–0 lead.

Harris fumbled early in the fourth period, setting up a Viking threat, but Greene recovered Foreman's fumble near the goal line. Still, Pittsburgh was penned in, and Bobby Walden had to punt. Matt Blair blocked the punt, and Terry Brown recovered it for a Minnesota touchdown. Fred Cox missed the extra point, so the Steelers had a 9–6 lead with ten minutes remaining.

Bradshaw, who had often been criticized for not being an intelligent field general, showed his skill under pressure, moving the Steelers 66 yards in 11 plays, mixing rushes by Bleier and Harris with a 30-yard pass to tight end Larry Brown. He finished with a 4-yard touchdown pass to Brown. With the kick, the score stood at 16–6.

Mike Wagner's interception gave Pittsburgh the ball again, and Harris ate up the clock with running plays. On his final run he gained 15 yards, giving him a day's total of 158 yards on 34 carries, breaking the year-old Super Bowl record of Larry Csonka, 145 yards in 33 carries.

There were a lot of stars in the Pittsburgh locker room, but Andy Russell, the defensive captain, knew who the biggest star was. He awarded the game ball to Art Rooney, who had waited 44 years for a Steeler championship.

"This one is for the Chief," Russell said. "It's been a long time coming."

**Pittsburgh Steelers 21 —
Dallas Cowboys 17
January 18, 1976, at Miami**

The Battle of the Champions

For the first time, two former Super Bowl champions met in the chilly Orange Bowl on January 18, 1976. Pittsburgh, the 1975 winner, met Dallas, the 1972 winner. Their collision would produce one of the most exciting Super Bowl games in the first decade.

The Cowboys were the same fine organization, changing players when necessary but using modern scouting and training techniques to remain a winner. Tom Landry's team still relied on aggressive Roger Staubach at quarterback — in his remarkable pro career after his career as a Navy officer.

The Steelers were also pretty much the same as they had been in their Super Bowl championship the year before. There was one big difference: Lynn Swann was a regular now.

Swann was a graceful athlete from the University of Southern California who had come to the Steelers in 1974. Like resourceful Franco Harris, Swann was not exactly the hard-headed Steel City type. Swann was soft-spoken, intelligent — and had an active interest in ballet. (He later became a director of the Pittsburgh Ballet Theater.)

In his rookie year, Swann performed mostly with the speciality units, returning 41 punts for 577 yards, second in the league and the best in Steeler history.

But in 1975, Swann replaced Ron Shanklin at wide receiver and caught 49 passes for 781 yards and 11 touchdowns, which tied him for the league lead with Mel Gray of St. Louis. He was the extra ingredient for Terry Bradshaw, whose quarterbacking seemed to grow wiser the longer he played.

Pittsburgh roared through the regular season with a 12–2 record and then beat Baltimore and Oakland in the play-offs. Dallas actually finished behind St. Louis in the regular season with a 10–4 record. But then the Cowboys beat Minnesota on a last-second pass from Staubach to Drew Pearson, and then beat Los Angeles to qualify for Super Bowl X.

The excitement began right at the kickoff, when the Cowboys pulled a reverse that gained a few extra yards. Both Dallas and Pittsburgh stalled, however, and Bobby Walden went back to punt for the Steelers. He fumbled the snap and was tackled at his own 29-yard line.

Staubach rushed in, eager to catch the Steelers while they were stunned. Drew Pearson, a lithe wide receiver, cut across the secondary for a quick 29-yard touchdown play and a 7–0 lead.

Now it was time for Swann's balletlike skills. He went high in the air over Mark Washington to complete a 36-yard play from Bradshaw. After dependable Rocky Bleier and Harris gained some yards on the ground, Randy Grossman, a reserve tight end, faked a block and slipped into the end zone for Bradshaw's 7-yard touchdown pass that tied the score.

Toni Fritsch kicked a 36-yard field goal that gave Dallas a 10–7 lead in the second period, and nobody scored for the next 33 minutes, as both defenses tightened.

However, the action got hot in the fourth period. Reggie Harrison, a sub running back who performed on Pittsburgh's specialty teams, blocked Mitch Hoopes's punt out of the end zone for a safety.

Now Dallas led by only a point, 10–9, and also had to kick off from its 20-yard line. Mike Collier ran it back 25 yards, setting up a 36-yard field goal by Roy Gerela that put the Steelers ahead, 12–10.

The scores came faster now. Mike Wagner intercepted a Staubach pass over the middle and ran it back 19 yards, setting up an easy 18-yard field goal by Gerela.

The Cowboys had to give up the ball, hoping their defense could pin the Steelers back. It almost worked, as Bradshaw was faced with a third-and-6 play on his own 36-yard line.

Hoping to set up a fumble or interception that could put them ahead, the Cowboys gambled with a double blitz, sending linebacker D. D. Lewis and free safety Cliff Harris after Bradshaw.

It almost worked. Lewis tackled Bradshaw legally a split second after he had released the ball. Bradshaw was knocked unconscious, but the ball soared upfield anyway.

Mark Washington, left alone with Swann because of the blitz, tried to stay with the leaper, but Swann caught the pass over his shoulder and raced into the end zone with a 64-yard touchdown that put the Steelers ahead, 21–10.

Staubach, who had pulled out many a game for Dallas since leaving the Navy, nearly did it again. As the 80,187 fans roared, he drove for a touchdown in just 62 seconds, scoring with a 34-yard touchdown pass to Percy Howard.

The Steelers had the ball but could not move. With 1:33 left, Chuck Noll, the coach, ordered Rocky Bleier to run on fourth-and-nine, hoping to use up time and make a first down. The run failed; the Steeler defense had to hold.

The famed "Steel Curtain" put on the pressure as Staubach moved for two first downs. But a last-second desperation pass was picked off by Glen Edwards. "That was beautiful, what Noll did," said defensive end L. C. Greenwood. "He turned the game over to us. The whole darn season, everything we had worked for since July, was on the line. And he left it up to us."

The Steelers had won the first battle of former champs, 21–17, and Swann's 161 yards on four receptions set a Super Bowl record for most yards by a receiver.

**Oakland Raiders 32 —
Minnesota Vikings 14
January 9, 1977, at Pasadena**

The Vikings Try Again

The Minnesota Vikings set a Super Bowl record in January of 1977 by becoming the first team to appear in four Super Bowls. That should have made the Vikings and their fans happy except for one thing — they had not yet won a Super Bowl.

Bud Grant's teams had been beaten in 1970, 1974, and 1975. Critics had found dozens of reasons for the Vikings' failures, but the basic answer was that the other team had been better on each of those Super Sundays. Now the Vikings had another chance.

This time their opponents were the Oakland Raiders, defeated in Super Bowl II. The Raiders were owned, operated, and very tightly supervised by Al Davis, the executive who had forced the merger of the AFL and the NFL back in 1966.

Davis had been stung when the New York Jets, not the Oakland Raiders, became the first AFL team to win a Super Bowl. Now here was a second chance for the Raiders. In the 1976 season, Oakland ran up a 13–1 record and then beat New England and Pittsburgh in the play-offs.

Minnesota had an 11–2–1 record during the regular season and then rolled over Washington and Los Angeles. The two teams met in front of 104,438 fans at the Rose Bowl in Pasadena on January 9, 1977, with a national television audience of 81 million watching.

The Oakland coach was John Madden — the same beefy fellow with the flapping arms who now appears on television in beer commercials and as a sports announcer.

Madden and Davis had a plan for the Vikings. The right side of Minnesota's defense appeared open to attack because of three relatively old and light players: end Jim Marshall, aged 39 and only 220 pounds; linebacker Wally Hilgenberg, age 34 and 220 pounds; and cornerback Bobby Bryant, age 32 and 170 pounds.

The Raiders planned to send their backs running behind the left side of the offensive line: tight end Dave Casper, 240; tackle Art Shell, 290; and guard Gene Upshaw, 260. Upshaw was a natural leader who later would become a power in the players' association. He was eager to earn the Super Bowl ring that he had missed as a rookie in the Super Bowl II loss.

The plan was simple, brutal — and effective. The Raiders survived an early scare when the Vikings' Fred McNeill blocked a punt by Ray Guy. Minnesota was within two yards of a touchdown, but Phil Villapiano knocked the ball away from running back Brent McClanahan, and Oakland's Willie Hall recovered. That was the only break Oakland needed.

Quarterback Ken (Snake) Stabler gave the ball to running backs Mark van Eeghen, Pete Banaszak, and Clarence Davis, who swerved left behind the big linemen. Errol Mann kicked a field goal, Casper caught a one-yard touchdown pass, and Banaszak ran a yard for a 16–0 halftime lead.

Mann made it 19–0 with a 40-yard field goal in the third period before Tarkenton engineered a 12-play, 58-yard drive that ended with an 8-yard scoring pass to Sammy White.

But Oakland came back for two touchdowns. Following an interception by Hall, Stabler threw a long pass to Fred Bilentnikoff when a Minnesota defender missed a coverage. Then Stabler handed off to Banaszak for a 2-yard touchdown run.

Willie Brown intercepted a Tarkenton pass for a 75-yard touchdown jaunt before substitute quarterback Bobby Lee passed to Stu Voigt for a meaningless Minnesota touchdown. The Raiders won, 32–14, and the Vikings had set another Super Bowl record by losing all four games.

SUPER BOWL XII

**Dallas Cowboys 27 —
Denver Broncos 10
January 15, 1978, at New Orleans**

*Staubach and
Morton Meet*

When Don Meredith, the last active member of the Dallas Cowboys expansion franchise of 1960, retired as quarterback on July 5, 1969, his heir apparent had been Craig Morton, his understudy for four years.

But Morton was beaten out after two years by Roger Staubach, the former Navy All-American, and Morton later moved to other teams. On January 15, 1978, Morton had a chance to beat Dallas and Staubach in the Super Bowl.

By this time, Morton had just helped the Denver Broncos win their first division title in their 18th season in pro football.

The Broncos had turned in the best record in the American Conference, 12 victories and two losses, which was one game better than the defending champions, the Raiders. The Broncos then beat Pittsburgh and Oakland—not a bad combination—to qualify for the Super Bowl.

The new Super Bowl contender was coached by Red Miller, in his first year as head coach. He had put together a strong defense known as the "Orange Crush" that had fans in Mile High Stadium waving orange banners. The Denver defense allowed only 148 points, the third lowest total in the league in the 1977 season.

The Denver fans brought their orange paraphernalia to the Superdome in New Orleans for Super Bowl XII. The Broncos would meet the Cowboys, who were appearing in their fourth Super Bowl, thus tying the Vikings for number of appearances.

The Cowboys had also won 12 games and lost two, and then had blasted the Chicago Bears, 37–7, and Minnesota, 23–6. The low scores for the opponents were an accurate indication of the Cowboys' defense.

How good was the Cowboys' defense? If you got past the monsters on the front line and the brutes at linebacker, you merely had to deal with two tough cornerbacks and safeties named Charlie Waters and Cliff Harris, two of the hardest tacklers in history.

Morton was a good passer, but he was not quick on his feet, which would soon become apparent to an estimated 102 million television viewers plus a sellout crowd of 75,583 in the indoor stadium.

"We knew we had to pressure Morton and upset him to win," said Randy White, a Dallas lineman.

The pressure began immediately, with Dallas sacking Morton for an 11-yard loss. Then linemen Harvey Martin and Randy White chased Morton until he tossed a wobbly pass that cornerback Randy Hughes intercepted. Five plays later, Tony Dorsett, the Cowboys' young star from the University of Pittsburgh, scored a 3-yard touchdown.

Efren Herrera kicked field goals of 35 and 43 yards for a 13-0 Dallas lead at halftime. Denver fumbled twice and Morton was intercepted two more times by the half.

In the second half, Jim Turner, the kicking star of the Jets' Super Bowl III victory, kicked a 47-yard field goal. But Butch Johnson made a diving fingertip catch of a Staubach pass as Johnson landed in the end zone for a 45-yard touchdown.

After Ed ("Too Tall") Jones nearly intercepted Morton, Red Miller sent in Norris Weese to replace Morton. Weese directed a touchdown drive to make the score 20-10, but Dallas had a surprise waiting for the Orange Crush defense.

After cornerback Aaron Kyle recovered a Weese fumble, Staubach handed off the ball to fullback Robert Newhouse. A probing run? That's what the Broncos thought.

Instead, Newhouse swept to his left, paused, and saw receiver Golden Richards alone near the end zone. Given the option to run or pass, Newhouse unleashed his first pass in three years, a 29-yard touchdown play to account for the final 27–10 score.

Randy White and Harvey Martin were chosen the Most Valuable Players in the game, but the reporters who voted could have picked the entire Dallas defense. The Cowboys tied Green Bay, Miami, and Pittsburgh as two-time winners of the 12-year-old event. And although the Cowboys weren't thinking about it in their jubilant clubhouse, a showdown with Pittsburgh was only 371 days away.

SUPER BOWL XIII

**Pittsburgh Steelers 35 —
Dallas Cowboys 31
January 21, 1979, at Miami**

A Classic from Double Champions

After two relatively one-sided games, the Super Bowl was overdue for a classic encounter, and it happened in Super Bowl XIII. This was the second Super Bowl battle between two of the double champions, the Pittsburgh Steelers and the Dallas Cowboys, both featuring many of the same players who had helped win two earlier Super Bowls.

Pittsburgh still had Terry Bradshaw, Franco Harris, and the Steel Curtain defense. Dallas still had Roger Staubach, unafraid to run the ball when he couldn't throw it, and those big, mobile defenders. And Chuck Noll and Tom Landry were still directing their teams' fortunes.

Pittsburgh had a better season record: 14–2 compared to Dallas's 12–4. In the play-offs, Pittsburgh romped over Denver and Houston while Dallas was beating Atlanta and Los Angeles. Then the two

66

former champions collided head-on in Miami's Orange Bowl and produced one of the best Super Bowls ever played.

Pittsburgh came out smoking and scored on its first possession as Bradshaw threw a 26-yard touchdown pass to John Stallworth. The Cowboys tied the game late in the first period when Staubach threw a 39-yard touchdown to Tony Hill.

After three minutes of the second quarter, Bradshaw dropped back to pass and was rushed by Harvey Martin and Randy White, the two defenders who had shared the vote as Most Valuable Players in Super Bowl XII.

Bradshaw, not known for his running, tried to avoid the two linemen but ran right into a blitzing linebacker, Thomas ("Hollywood") Henderson. Henderson had acquired his nickname because of his boasting in the two-week period before the game. His antics were hardly in the style of his closemouthed coach, Tom Landry, but nobody on Dallas objected to his violent tackle of Bradshaw on this play.

As soon as Henderson grasped Bradshaw, another blitzing linebacker, Mike Hegman, roared in and took the ball from Bradshaw and raced 37 yards for a touchdown. Meanwhile, Henderson's tackle hurt Bradshaw's shoulder.

"It scared me to death," Bradshaw said later. "When the doctor first checked it, he said I had a separated shoulder. I about had a fit. But it felt better fast, and I went back in."

Down by a touchdown, Bradshaw came back and threw a 10-yard pass to Stallworth, who cut inside a block by Lynn Swann for a 75-yard touchdown play.

Rocky Bleier, the rugged Steeler running back who had been injured in the Vietnam war, made a spectacular play with 26 seconds left in the half. Bradshaw lofted a pass just behind the linebacker, D. D. Lewis, and Bleier caught it with his fingertips for a 7-yard touchdown that put Pittsburgh ahead, 21–14, at the half.

Bradshaw had a superb first half in passing. Then he had trouble with the Cowboys' extra defensive backs in the third period as the two teams slugged at each other like champions. But late in the third quarter, the Steelers got a break.

Staubach had moved the Cowboys to the Steeler 10-yard line. Apparently looking for more blocking for their running plays, the Cowboys brought in an extra tight end, 38-year-old Jackie Smith, who had been persuaded to come out of retirement for the 1977 season.

As the Steelers bunched up for the run, Smith looped into the end zone and Staubach lofted a soft pass toward him. But the ball fell through Smith's hands, costing a sure touchdown. The Cowboys had to settle for Rafael Septien's 27-yard field goal.

Dallas stopped Pittsburgh for two series, but the third time Pittsburgh got another break. Swann cut back for an underthrown pass, fell in a tangle with Dallas cornerback Benny Barnes, and was given a pass-interference call by the field judge, who was positioned upfield. Many people disagreed with the call, but it gave Pittsburgh 33 yards and a first down on the Cowboy 31.

Running on third down, Franco Harris stunned the Cowboys with a 22-yard touchdown run for a 28–17 lead.

On the kickoff, Roy Gerela squibbed the ball unintentionally, and Randy White tried to pick it up at the 25-yard line. But White's hand was in a cast, and he fumbled the ball and Dennis Winston recovered for Pittsburgh.

On first down, Bradshaw caught the Cowboys again, tossing an 18-yard touchdown pass to Swann for a 35–17 lead with 6:51 remaining.

Staubach, who had engineered many a winning march in the final quarter, now tried to produce a miracle. He moved the Cowboys to the Steelers' 8-yard line, and tight end Billy Joe DuPree took a pass and bulled his way for a touchdown.

Septien kicked short on purpose, and the Cowboys' Dennis Thurman outfought the Steelers for the ball on the Cowboys' 48-yard line. Two long completions to Drew Pearson brought the Cowboys close. Then Staubach threw a 4-yard touchdown to Butch Johnson.

Now the margin was only four points, but Dallas needed the ball again. Septien tried an onside kick, but Rocky Bleier, who had known worse combat than on a football field, dove for the loose ball that guaranteed the Steelers their third Super Bowl title. The final score was 35–31.

"It took the best to beat the best," said Pittsburgh's Joe Greene. And the 79,484 fans filing limply out of the Orange Bowl would have agreed with that.

SUPER BOWL XIV

**Pittsburgh Steelers 31—
Los Angeles Rams 19
January 20, 1980, at Pasadena**

The Rams Come Close

In the tenth game of the 1979 season, quarterback Pat Haden broke the pinky on his throwing hand when he caught it in the seam of the artificial turf in Seattle's Kingdome.

That break could have doomed the Los Angeles Rams' chances for the year, but it didn't. Instead of Haden, a former Rhodes Scholar and current law student at quarterback, the Rams now had a former medical student named Vince Ferragamo. And suddenly they were in the Super Bowl against the only three-time champions, the Pittsburgh Steelers.

The Steelers had won three Super Bowls all with one quarterback. The Rams always seemed to have at least two quarterbacks, an odd tradition that led to great controversy.

In their early years, they had two great quarterbacks, Bob Waterfield and Norm Van Brocklin, sharing the job. Later it was a dizzying combination of Billy Wade, Frank Ryan, Bill Munson, Roman Gabriel, John Hadl, James Harris, Ron Jaworski, and even rickety-kneed Joe Namath after his years with the Jets. The Rams just collected quarterbacks the way other people stock up on television sets: one for every room.

Still, the swarthily handsome Ferragamo came in handy when Haden went out for the year. Although blessed with a powerful throwing arm, Ferragamo was not considered experienced enough to call plays for a championship team. The Rams finished with a 9–7 record and then upset Dallas, 21–19, and beat Tampa Bay, 9–0.

It had been a troubled year for the Los Angeles franchise. In April, their owner, Carroll Rosenbloom, had drowned while swimming in heavy surf near his home in Florida. Then his new wife, Georgia, had fought with Rosenbloom's son, Steve, over control of the club until she managed to force him out of the picture.

Coach Ray Malavasi often seemed in a shaky position, with 13 starting players injured at one time or another. Most of them were hurting on the eve of Super Bowl XIV at the Rose Bowl.

Jack Youngblood, playing with a hairline fracture of his right leg, said, "You know, there are people bad-mouthing us, saying that we are lucky, that we shouldn't be here, that we're not worthy of the opponent. Well, we are worthy. And we're going to prove it against the Steelers."

The Steelers, who had a 12–4 record during the season and beat Miami and Houston in the play-offs, scored first against the Rams when Matt Bahr kicked a 41-yard field goal.

But the Rams roared back for a touchdown after recovering an onside kick by the Steelers. Ferragamo completed a pass to running back Wendell Tyler for six yards and then came back with a sweep to the left by Tyler. The back gained 39 yards before Pittsburgh could stop him.

Shortly afterward, Cullen Bryant barrelled in for a touchdown from the 1-yard line for a 7–3 Ram lead.

Franco Harris scored on a 1-yard touchdown run to put the Steelers ahead, but Frank Corral kicked a 31-yard field goal to tie. Then, late in the first half, Malavasi allowed Ferragamo to pass on fourth-and-8 at the Steeler 37-yard line instead of kicking. Ferragamo completed a clutch pass to Billy Waddy, and Corral later got within range for a 45-yard field goal.

Bradshaw threw a 47-yard touchdown pass to Lynn Swann in the third period, but the Rams came back to score again when Lawrence Mc-Cutcheon, a running back, threw an option pass to Ron Smith for a 24-yard touchdown.

The extra point failed, so with one quarter to go, Ferragamo and the Rams led, 19–17.

But Bradshaw and John Stallworth pulled off a 73-yard touchdown play, with Stallworth drawing defensive backs Rod Perry and Dave Elmendorf to him, then taking off downfield and catching Bradshaw's long bomb.

Down by five, Ferragamo began a long march that threatened the champions. But the veteran linebacker, Jack Lambert, read a pass perfectly and intercepted with 5:24 left.

Once again the Rams made a mistake on defensive coverage and Stallworth got behind the backs for a 45-yard gain. Bradshaw moved the team close enough for Franco Harris' 1-yard touchdown run that clinched a 31–19 victory. Many people had not expected that much.

The Steelers had their fourth Super Bowl title in four tries. The Rams were 0 for 1 in Super Bowls, but as tackle Larry Brooks put it: "Who in the world would say we didn't play admirably?"

Green Bay's Donny Anderson (44) goes for some yardage. The Packers won over the Oakland Raiders 33—14 in Super Bowl II (1968)

Jets quarterback, Joe Namath (12), whose passing arm, boasts about winning ("The Mouth that Roared"), and steady running game won Super Bowl III for Jets over favored Colts.

With good team blocking against Minnesota Vikings, Kansas City quarterback Len Dawson (16) gets off a pass early in first quarter of Super Bowl IV. (UPI)

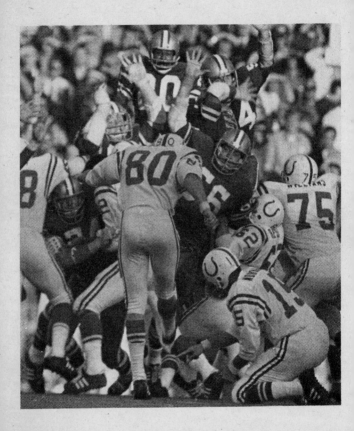

Baltimore's Jim O'Brien (80) kicks winning field goal in closing seconds of Super Bowl V. (UPI)

After Miami Yepremian's field goal was blocked by Redskins, the ball bounced back into his hands. The little placekicker then tried to pass the ball; it was deflected by Redskins' Bass (41), who scored Redskins' only touchdown in Super Bowl VII. (Wide World)

Terry Bradshaw (12) holds up "number one" fingers as he walks off the field after Pittsburgh's third victory in the Super Bowl, a record they would clinch with a fourth win in 1980. (UPI)

Swann repeats last year's flying catch. Soaring high to grab Bradshaw's pass from between Rams' defenders in the third quarter of Super Bowl XIV, he gained 47 yards on a touchdown play. (UPI)

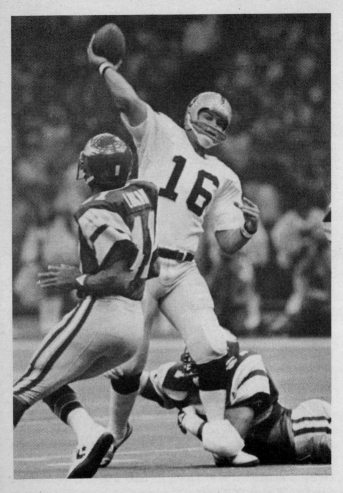

Oakland's Jim Plunkett flips a short pass downfield, incomplete as Eagles' Logan (41) puts pressure on him in first quarter. Oakland won Super Bowl XV, 27—10. (UPI)

Bill Walsh, 49ers' coach, receives congratu-
lations from President Reagan after 49ers won
Super Bowl XVI over the Bengals. (Walsh
coached the Bengals before moving to San
Francisco.) (Wide World). (below) Ronnie Lott
(42) leads cheering section after 49ers stopped
the Bengals on a goal line in third quarter.
(UPI)

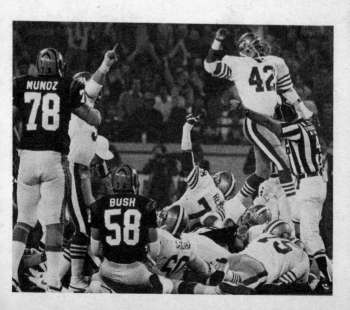

Washington's running back, John Riggins, breaks away for winning touchdown against Miami in Super Bowl XVII. (UPI)

Marcus Allen, former Heisman Trophy winner, looks for a hole in the Washington line during the first half of Super Bowl XVIII. (AP/Wide World)

Los Angeles Raiders' punter Ray Guy stretches for a high snap in Super Bowl XVIII. Guy got off a successful punt to the Washington Redskins, who lost to Los Angeles, 38–9. (AP/Wide World)

MVP quarterback Joe Montana (16) of the San Francisco 49ers, goes down in the end zone for a touchdown during Super Bowl XIX. The Miami Dolphins defender is Lyle Blackwood (42). San Francisco went on to beat Miami, 38–16. (UPI/Bettmann Newsphotos)

The Chicago Bears' William Perry explodes into the end zone for six points against the New England Patriots in Super Bowl XX. (AP/Wide World)

Quarterback Jim McMahon and Walter Payton (34) of Chicago sport their headbands on the sidelines of Super Bowl XX. Payton was disappointed that he didn't get a chance to score in the Bears' romp against New England. (AP/Wide World)

Matt Suhey dives across the goal line to score the first touchdown for Chicago in Super Bowl XX. New England Patriots' Fred Marion follows Suhey into the end zone. (below) Winning head coach Mike Ditka is carried off the field on the hefty shoulders of Steve McMichael (left) and William Perry. His victorious Bear escorts are Willie Gault (83) and Maury Buford (8). (AP/Wide World)

SUPER BOWL XV

Oakland Raiders 27 —
Philadelphia Eagles 10
January 25, 1981, at New Orleans

Back from the Brink

Jim Plunkett had thought his career was over several times, but on January 25, 1981, he found himself playing quarterback for the Oakland Raiders in Super Bowl XV.

By a strange irony, Plunkett, who is half Mexican and half Irish, was playing for Tom Flores, the first Mexican-American coach in the history of the NFL. And a further irony was that the rival coach in the Super Bowl, Dick Vermeil of the Philadelphia Eagles, had been the coach of the quarterbacks when Plunkett attended Stanford University.

The Eagles had come a long way under Vermeil to reach the Super Bowl. But nobody had come further than Jim Plunkett. Once a college star and the leading rookie in the NFL with the New England Patriots, he had been traded by the Patriots and released by the San Francisco 49ers early in 1978.

"I felt like the whole world was caving in on me," Plunkett admitted later. "I hung around home and didn't go out at all. I had trouble sleeping."

The Raiders had hired him strictly as a second-string quarterback, and that only after a physical inspection and an Al Davis-ordered cut in pay, which made Plunkett doubt his own future. Nobody expected him to beat out Dan Pastorini, whom the Raiders had acquired from Houston in a controversial trade for Ken Stabler.

Davis told Plunkett to "learn the system and get adjusted." There was certainly time for all of that. Plunkett did not throw one pass in 1978 and threw only 15 in 1979. But in the fifth game of the 1980 season, Pastorini's leg was broken in a game against Kansas City. As a replacement, Plunkett was sacked five times and threw five interceptions. But he played quarterback the following week because there was nobody else.

Oakland won nine and lost two with Plunkett at quarterback and barely qualified for the playoffs with a wild-card spot that forced them to play an extra round. But the Raiders were a rugged, confident team, with natural leaders like linemen Gene Upshaw and John Matuszak.

Flores, a quiet coach from the farmland of the San Joaquin Valley, had become head coach when John Madden gave up coaching. Al Davis was still masterminding the team's major decisions, of course.

In the play-offs, the Raiders knocked off three teams with good quarterbacks: Houston with Stabler, Cleveland with Brian Sipe, and San Diego with Dan Fouts. Plunkett had regained his confidence, and Vermeil knew he would be dangerous.

Vermeil was a hard-working coach who was known to sleep in his office rather than waste time driving home for a few hours of sleep between watching films and practice. He had built a formidable team with a pretty good quarterback, Ron Jaworski.

Vermeil tried to maintain the tight discipline as he led the Eagles to their first Super Bowl in the raucous city of New Orleans. He ordered them to remain confined to their hotels rather than go out on the town. The Raiders were less confined, but they did have a curfew. John Matuszak, the boisterous defensive lineman, decided that a night on the town was worth a fine, so he went partying and paid the cost. The Eagles had discipline; the Raiders had fun.

The crowd in the Superdome of New Orleans had barely gotten settled when Rod Martin of Oakland intercepted a Jaworski pass. Plunkett moved the Raiders downfield, until they were third-and-goal on the Eagles' 2-yard line.

Instead of going for a rush, Plunkett faked a handoff and dropped back to pass. Two Eagles converged on him, but he stepped forward and fired a 2-yard scoring pass to Cliff Branch.

Later in the first period, Plunkett made an audacious play under fire. Scrambling to his left and moving as he threw, he lofted the ball over Herman Edwards, an Eagle cornerback, to Kenny King. King completed the 80-yard touchdown play, the longest play from scrimmage in Super Bowl history.

Tony Franklin scored a 30-yard field goal to make the score 14–3 at halftime, but early in the third period, Plunkett threw a 29-yard touchdown to Branch. It was the second touchdown of the day for Branch, a speedy veteran from Colorado.

Chris Bahr kicked a field goal to make it 24–3 before Jaworski threw a touchdown to Keith Krepfle. Bahr finished the scoring with a field goal to make it 27–10 in favor of Oakland. Martin's record-setting three interceptions were the outstanding defensive statistic, and Plunkett's 13-of-21 for 261 yards earned him the Most Valuable Player award for Super Bowl XV.

After the game, the boisterous Raiders like Matuszak and Upshaw roared their happiness while the shy Plunkett sat in a corner, surrounded by reporters.

"I'm happy," he insisted. "Believe me. I'm just not very good at showing how I feel."

After the comeback he'd made, Plunkett certainly had every right to be very happy.

SUPER BOWL XVI

San Francisco 49ers 26 —
Cincinnati Bengals 21
January 24, 1982, at Pontiac, MI

Northern Exposure

The Super Bowl moved north for the first time in 1982. Instead of a warm-weather site in the middle of winter, the Super Bowl was held in Pontiac, Michigan, where the Detroit Lions play indoors at the Silverdome.

For most of the country, it didn't matter where the San Francisco 49ers were meeting the Cincinnati Bengals. Most people would watch the game on television.

But for anybody going to the Super Bowl, the site meant a difference. Instead of carrying golf clubs and tennis racquets, visitors brought snow boots and overcoats.

One visiting reporter, stuck in press headquarters in the middle of some shopping center out in the suburbs, described his location as "Siberia." For the rest of the week, he was getting telephone calls from angry Michigan residents.

Many other visitors muttered a few things about "Siberia," too, when the highways became clogged before gametime because a motorcade with Vice-President Bush arrived at the wrong time, so the fans had to trek through snowdrifts and icy parking lots in biting winds.

Even one of the 49er buses was hung up by the motorcade.

"Coach Walsh was pretty loose on the bus," quarterback Joe Montana joked later about Bill Walsh. "He said, 'I've got the radio on and we're leading, 7–0. The trainer's calling the plays.' "

Once indoors, it was 72 degrees with a one-mile-per-hour breeze floating through the giant, inflated dome. And two teams battled in the first Super Bowl for each.

Cincinnati had joined the old AFL in 1968, under Paul Brown, the master builder who had taken the Cleveland Browns from the old All-American Conference to the NFL.

Brown was the general manager of the Bengals in 1981, and he had hired a coach, Forrest Gregg, who had once played for the championship Green Bay Packers and Vince Lombardi. The Bengals relied upon quarterback Ken Anderson, from little-known Augustana College in Illinois.

Anderson had been discovered by the former Cincinnati assistant coach, Bill Walsh, on a scouting assignment. Walsh had lobbied hard to get Paul

Brown to draft him, and then Walsh had made Anderson his special project.

After building the Bengals' offense, Walsh had hoped to be head coach someday. But Paul Brown apparently did not think Walsh was tough enough to be a head coach, because he overlooked Walsh when the head job became available.

"I had aspirations for the Bengal job; I had hopes," Walsh said later. "But no bitterness on my part at all, only vast disappointment."

Walsh then returned home to California to coach at Stanford and finally received his first head coaching job in the NFL — with the San Francisco 49ers. There he took a scrappy ex-Notre Dame quarterback, Joe Montana, and installed him in a complex, wide-open passing offense.

In the 1981 season, the 49ers had the best record in the NFL — 13 victories and 3 losses. Then they outscored the New York Giants, 38–24, and edged Dallas, 28–27.

The Bengals beat Buffalo, 28–21, and then beat San Diego, 27–7, in Cincinnati, where the windchill factor was estimated at 54 degrees below zero. They didn't mind the weather outdoors in Pontiac, Michigan, at all — as long as the game would be played inside.

For the first half, it was all San Francisco, after Anderson was intercepted by Dwight Hicks on the 49ers' 5-yard line. Montana picked the Bengals apart on a 68-yard drive, scoring on a 1-yard run. Then Montana engineered the longest scoring drive in Super Bowl history — 92 yards in 12 plays, with Earl Cooper taking an 11-yard touchdown pass at the end.

Ray Wersching, a nine-year veteran, kicked 22- and 26-yard field goals in the first half, allowing the 49ers to come off the field with a 20–0 lead.

In the Bengal dressing room, rugged Forrest Gregg had a very simple halftime talk.

"I just told 'em it was about time we played a little football," he said later.

Bill Walsh had created a monster in Ken Anderson. Walsh's former protégé went to work after halftime, moving 83 yards in nine plays, finishing with a 5-yard touchdown run.

The Bengals got the ball back and stormed downfield to the 49ers' 3-yard line. Then they sent Pete Johnson, their 250-pound fullback, into the middle of the line. Once, twice, three times, four times, Johnson could not get past a superb goal-line team of the 49ers, and a vital drive had been lost.

The Bengals' defense got the ball back, and Anderson moved 53 yards in seven plays, with a 4-yard touchdown pass to Dan Ross. Now the 49ers' lead was only 20–14.

Wersching kicked two more field goals, of 40 and 23 yards, in the fourth period to widen the lead again. But Anderson struck back for a 74-

yard drive, ending in a 3-yard touchdown pass to Ross.

The 49ers hung on for a 26–21 victory, but they admitted it had not been easy. Cincinnati gained 356 yards to San Francisco's 275, the first time in 16 Super Bowls that the losers had outgained the winners.

For Anderson, both his 25 completions and his completion percentage of 73.5 percent were records in Super Bowl history. And Ross set a Super Bowl record with 11 receptions for 104 yards.

"I've got mixed emotions about all this," Ross said. "It's nice that I set the record, but there's an empty feeling. A great disappointment. We came so far — from a team that was 6–10 last year — and then we just miss winning the biggest game of the year."

But Montana was voted the game's Most Valuable Player for completing 14 of 22 for 157 yards and giving the 49ers the big halftime lead.

All in all, it was not a bad day for the two quarterbacks — and for the silver-haired Bill Walsh, who had coached them both.

SUPER BOWL XVII

**Washington Redskins 27—
Miami Dolphins 17
January 30, 1983, at Pasadena**

Hog Power

Offensive linemen are the unsung foot soldiers of football. They are stocky and not particularly speedy athletes who block for the glamorous players trusted to handle the ball. They don't even have the emotional release of occasionally "sacking" a quarterback or forcing an enemy fumble, the way their teammates do on the defensive side.

Instead, offensive linemen follow orders and run their plays. They often last longer than players at any other position, but rarely do offensive linemen become celebrities.

In Washington during the 1982 season, however, a strange thing happened. Offensive linemen became heroes. Television announcers flocked to their lockers. Reporters asked for their life stories. Fans asked for their autographs and even made banners and cheered for them — by name!

The Washington offensive linemen had gained fame and a nickname in 1981, when a new coach,

Joe Gibbs, brought in Joe Bugel as offensive line coach. Bugel described his new charges as "short with big bellies," and he began addressing them as Hogs.

At summer camp in 1982, Bugel had T-shirts ready for the linemen in the Redskins' familiar colors of white, burgundy, and gold. On the chest was a sketch of a ferocious hog, standing between goalposts. If the Hogs didn't wear the shirt to midweek practice, they were fined $5. The money went to buy more food for team parties, where the Hogs ordered one large pizza per man, and talked football. They were proud and protective of their nickname.

The Head Hog was George Starke, a 34-year-old graduate of Columbia University, a school that is known for producing more poets than professional linemen. He was in charge of membership in the Hogs.

"Lots of lobbying going on," Starke said. "But you just can't let everybody in."

Only bona-fide blockers were allowed to be Hogs: Russ Grimm, Jeff Bostic, Joe Jacoby, Mark May, Fred Dean, Ron Saul, and Starke from the interior line and two tight ends, Don Warren and Rick Walker.

Then early in the 1982 season, the Hogs extended an invitation to John Riggins, the burly running back of the Redskins.

Riggins had been something of a character in his early days with the New York Jets, affecting a Mohawk haircut and wearing leather vests over his bare chest. He quit the Redskins after the 1979 season to stay home on his Kansas farm, but Joe Gibbs talked him into returning for 1981. Riggins greeted players and press with the terse statement, "I'm bored, I'm broke — and I'm back."

Riggins was so powerful at crashing into the line that the Hogs recognized him as a "blue-collar workman, just like us," as center Jeff Bostic explained it.

They would not allow Joe Theismann, the talkative quarterback, into their group. The wide receivers formed their own group, "the Fun Bunch," who celebrated touchdowns by leaping into the air like a team of sky divers in reverse. Another group of small specialty players called themselves "Smurfs," after the cuddly, furry toy.

The defensive unit didn't have a name, but it wasn't bad, either. It helped the Redskins win eight of nine games in a strike-shortened season, and then score one-sided victories over Detroit, Minnesota, and hated Dallas in the play-offs.

The Redskins' opponent in the Super Bowl would be the Miami Dolphins, the team that had beaten Washington in Super Bowl VII. By the 1982 season, Dolphin coach Don Shula was in his 20th season as a head coach — and in his fifth Super Bowl, tying him with Tom Landry of Dallas for most appearances.

Shula had rebuilt the Dolphins following the defection of three key players to the short-lived World Football League and the loss of several other players to drug problems. In 1982 he alternated David Woodley, 23, and Don Strock, 32, at quarterback until people began calling them "Woodstrock," a name Shula hated.

Woodley led the Dolphins through play-off victories over New England, San Diego, and the Jets. Then it was on to Southern California. A series of coastal storms pounded the fragile beaches, piers, hills, and homes; and there were fears that the Rose Bowl might turn into the Mud Bowl on Super Sunday.

The Hogs found themselves bored with the routine of Super Bowl week. They staged a late-night pizza party, spending several hundred dollars on their favorite food. On Friday night, the Redskins' owner, Jack Kent Cooke, threw a party. Riggins did not show up in a leather vest, jeans, and boots as he might have done in his old rebel days. He showed up in a tuxedo and top hat.

The day of the Super Bowl dawned bright and clear. The National Football League and the Super Bowl did not get to be a billion-dollar enterprise without a little bit of luck.

The Dolphins scored first, as Woodley threw a

76-yard pass to Jimmy Cefalo, the young receiver from Penn State who was looking forward to a career in broadcasting. For a second time, the Hogs could not move the team, but after a punt, Dexter Manley forced Woodley to fumble the ball away to Dave Butz. Riggins lugged the ball close enough for Mark Moseley to kick a 31-yard field goal.

Miami struck quickly again. Fulton Walker, a little-known back, ran the kickoff back 42 yards, and Uwe von Schamann, from West Germany and Oklahoma, kicked a 20-yard field goal to make it 10–3, Miami.

Theismann ran an imaginative series of plays that included a 27-yard completion to Rick Walker; a reverse run by Walker; a scrambling 15-yard completion to Riggins; and a four-yard touchdown pass to Alvin Garrett, one of the Smurfs.

The game was tied briefly until Fulton Walker ran the kickoff back 98 yards for the longest play of any kind in Super Bowl history. The first half ended with Miami leading, 17–10, and Theismann running out of time on the Dolphins' nine. The crowd knew it was seeing one of the most exciting Super Bowl games yet.

Moseley kicked a 20-yard field goal in the third period, but Theismann was having all kinds of trouble with Miami's unheralded defenders, known as the Killer Bees because seven of their last names began with "B." At one point, Theismann's pass was deflected by tall Kim Bokamper, and Theismann had to leap high in the air to spike the ball out of Bokamper's hands, to avoid an interception and possible touchdown.

Undaunted, Theismann tried a flea-flicker play. The ball went from Theismann to Riggins and back to Theismann, who threw a pass that was intercepted by Lyle Blackwood of the Bees.

Woodley, however, could not move the Dolphins, and Miami had to punt to the Redskins. This time the Hogs were ready. They charged to the Dolphins' 43, where Otis Wonsley, an unsung blocking back, led the way for Riggins on fourth down and one. With Joe Jacoby, the 290-pound tackle, making a big block, Riggins broke into the secondary. He broke a belated tackle by Don McNeal, who had slipped earlier in the play, and rumbled for the touchdown that put the Redskins ahead.

"I got my arms around him but he slipped away," McNeal lamented later. "He was like a train."

In the final minutes, neither half of "Woodstrock" could move the Dolphins, and Riggins set up a six-yard scoring pass from Theismann to Charlie Brown for the final score in the 27–17 victory. The Redskins had won their first league championship since 1942, as Riggins set Super Bowl records by rushing 38 times for 166 yards. In the four postseason games, the big man from the plains of Kansas had gained 610 yards, an incredible effort against the best defenses in the league.

Each Dolphin had been paid $18,000 for reaching the Super Bowl, but the Redskins earned $36,000 per man for winning. As far as the Hogs were concerned, that would buy a lot of pizza.

SUPER BOWL XVIII

**Los Angeles Raiders 38—
Washington Redskins 9
January 22, 1984, at Tampa**

The Raiders Take Over

People arriving for Super Bowl XVIII were confronted by billboards all around the Tampa Bay area of Florida. There were 112 billboards that said, "Commitment to Excellence," and a few others that said, "You Are Now Entering Raider Land."

Most visitors shrugged off the billboards, but the Washington Redskins' fans were not amused. Their team was about to play Al Davis's black-and-silver-clad warriors, and they had the feeling Davis had already turned Tampa into a Raider sanctuary.

Their feelings were reinforced at the game. Somebody from the Raiders' organization had recruited students and nuns from a local parochial high school to pass out black-and-silver pom-poms to fans entering the stadium.

The Raiders were very good at moving into a town and making it their own. By Super Bowl

XVIII, the Raiders were more than ever the renegades of the National Football League, having abandoned Oakland after two highly successful decades there.

When they won Super Bowl XV at New Orleans in 1981, Davis had already established offices in Los Angeles. But various court decisions kept the Raiders playing in Oakland until a favorable decision in 1982 allowed the Raiders to move down the coast to Los Angeles, filling the gap left by the Rams' move to Anaheim Stadium in Orange County.

Had this game of musical chairs affected the Raiders? Perhaps. They were 14–5 in their Super Bowl XV season, but fell to 7–9 in 1981 while awaiting permission to move.

In 1982 the Los Angeles Raiders had an overall record of 9–2 in the strike-shortened season, losing to their old rivals, the Jets, in the play-offs. But in 1983, they had a 12–4 regular-season record, tying Dallas for second best in the league. Only the defending Super Bowl champions, the Washington Redskins, with a 14–2 record, did better. The Raiders and Redskins both won their two play-off games, setting up the meeting of former champions at Tampa.

The league was not exactly thrilled with the Raiders' presence, since Davis had a $34.6 million suit against the league for trying to keep him from moving his franchise. The issue is highly complicated, since cities like Oakland have contributed a great deal of tax money to build stadiums and roads to keep a team like the Raiders. But Davis's lawyers argued that there are antitrust laws that allow a business organization to move its base of operations. He would eventually win his suit, and in 1986 the U.S. Supreme Court would refuse to hear the league's appeal of a lower-court ruling.

For most fans, of course, there was more interest in the game on the field than the duel in the courts. Except for being a year older, the Redskins were much the same team that had won the Super Bowl the year before. The Raiders had done plenty of rebuilding since their last Super Bowl victory, but Davis and coach Tom Flores still stressed performance and intimidation ahead of details and finesse.

Davis had come up with a new terror in the classic Raider mold, Lyle Alzado, a former boxer from New York, who worked with Howie Long and Reggie Kinlaw in a three-man defensive line. Two all-pro cornerbacks, Lester Hayes and Mike Haynes, were experts in the Raiders' traditional tactic of bump-and-run coverage on wide receivers. The offense was still in the hands of Jim Plunkett, with Marcus Allen, the former Heisman Trophy winner from Southern California, the running threat.

The Tampa Bay area was the smallest metropolitan center ever to hold a Super Bowl. The region proved a good host, although it could do nothing about the brisk 20-mile-per-hour winds that cut through Tampa Stadium on game day.

The Raiders established themselves when the game was barely five minutes old. Derrick Jensen, the captain of their specialty teams, got around Otis Wonsley, the Redskins' dependable blocker, to smother a punt by Jeff Hayes and fall on the ball in the end zone for a 7–0 lead.

In the second period, Plunkett threw a 50-yard pass to Cliff Branch, the dependable receiver, and then threw a 12-yard scoring pass to Branch for a 14–0 lead.

Mark Moseley kicked a 24-yard field goal to give the Redskins a score, but then coach Joe Gibbs and quarterback Joe Theismann tried too hard to get the Redskins back on the board. With the Redskins on their own 12-yard line with 12 seconds left in the half, they both remembered Theismann throwing a screen pass to Joe Washington for a 60-yard touchdown during the Redskins' 37–35 victory over the Raiders during the regular season.

The only problem was, the Raiders also remembered. Their defensive coordinator, Charlie Sumner, sent in Jack Squirek, a linebacker who played mostly in obvious passing situations. Sumner told Squirek to watch out for the screen play. When Theismann lobbed the screen pass, Squirek cut in front of Joe Washington, caught the ball on the five-yard line, and broke into the end zone. The half ended with the Raiders leading, 21–3, and the Redskins in big trouble.

In the second half, the Redskins went back to basics. Theismann gained 50 yards on passes, and John Riggins, who often spent time in the hospital with his aching back in traction, ran six times for 30 yards. Riggins scored from the one-yard line, but Don Hasselbeck of the Raiders blocked the extra point, to keep the score at 21–9.

The Redskins' hopes faded fast. The Raiders moved too quickly for them, scoring on eight plays, with Allen running in from the five. On the last play of the third quarter, Allen raced toward the left side, saw the Redskins coming, and cut back to the right side. He even out-ran Darrell Green, one of the fastest men in the NFL, for a 74-yard touchdown, the longest in the history of the Super Bowl. The Raiders had a 35–9 lead.

"It was a foul-up, to be honest with you," Allen told reporters later. "I was supposed to go inside, but I went outside instead. Then I had to reverse myself, and I was off to the races."

In the final period, Chris Bahr of the Raiders kicked a 21-yard field goal as the crowd began to file out into the blustery evening. Television viewers stayed put, possibly to see whether there would be fireworks when commissioner Pete Rozelle had to present the Super Bowl trophy to Al Davis, the man with the multimillion-dollar lawsuit against the league.

In the crowded dressing room, the two men stood on a podium, and the trophy changed hands. There were no incidents, but not a lot of smiles and eye contact, either.

Winning coach Tom Flores became the first man to play for a champion (the Kansas City Chiefs of Super Bowl IV), coach a champion (the Oakland Raiders of Super Bowl XV), and win rings in two different cities, Oakland and Los Angeles. No matter where the Raiders played, they seemed to personify another favorite expression of Al Davis: "Just win, baby." He might put that on a few billboards, too.

San Francisco 49ers 38—
Miami Dolphins 16
January 20, 1985, at Palo Alto

The Quarterbacks from Pittsburgh

After losing to the Redskins in Super Bowl XVII, Miami coach Don Shula broke up the old "Woodstrock" quarterback combination that had helped the Dolphins reach the final game. David Woodley moved on to another team, and Don Strock became strictly a backup quarterback.

The new quarterback was a strong young man from the University of Pittsburgh named Dan Marino. With his powerful arm, he became a regular as a rookie, and in his second season he led the Dolphins back to the Super Bowl. There he was matched with the hero of Super Bowl XVI, Joe Montana of the San Francisco 49ers.

It was one of the classic match-ups in the history of the Super Bowl. Both quarterbacks were so good, yet so different, and both of them, coincidentally, had grown up in the Pittsburgh area. Montana was a mobile quarterback who could operate coach Bill Walsh's complex offense. Marino was the latest drop-back passer who could operate Don Shula's more straightforward offense.

The two teams dominated their conferences in the 1984 season. Miami had a 14–2 record, the best in the American Conference. San Francisco had a 15–1 record in the National Conference. Both teams won two play-off games by no fewer than 11 points and raced into the Super Bowl as the cream of the NFL for 1984.

The 49ers immmediately had an advantage. Since Super Bowl XIX was to be played at Stanford University in Palo Alto, California, just south of San Francisco, the 49ers were sure to have the crowd behind them.

As usual, Super Bowl headquarters were spread all over the host area: the Dolphins based in Oakland, the 49ers near the San Francisco airport, and the league officials and press in downtown San Francisco.

The focus of Super Bowl week was on San Francisco, with its picturesque cable cars, only recently renovated and back on the hills again. Some players found time away from practice to develop the fine art of hanging by one hand from a moving cable car and playing "chicken" with passengers on an approaching car.

Much of the pregame conversation centered around the two quarterbacks. Montana, the wiry

Notre Dame alumnus, had been in the league six years and thrown 106 touchdown passes. Marino, the muscular Pitt man, had thrown 68 touchdown passes in just two seasons.

Joe Namath, the star of Super Bowl III, was asked which quarterback he preferred in Super Bowl XIX. Namath, now working as an actor and a broadcaster, said:

"If I'm down to the wire with one game to go, I'll take Montana. He's got more experience, and he's got the arm and the legs. He's got much quicker feet than Marino has. He looks like Fred Astaire back there. But for throwing the ball, Marino throws it better than anybody I've ever seen. He's accurate. He's just the best passer I've ever seen."

It was hard to separate the quarterbacks from their coaches and their systems. Bill Walsh, with his multiple offenses and varied options, needed a quarterback who could stall and create until Dwight Clark and Freddie Solomon got free. Don Shula, with his set plays, was happy with a quarterback who could hit fleet Mark Duper and Mark Clayton on preplanned pass patterns.

In his first Super Bowl victory, Bill Walsh had been crowned a genius. Then the 49ers slumped badly during the strike season. Now Walsh was being hailed as a genius again, and his reputation almost, just almost, seemed to make Don Shula sizzle.

Shula, who had won two of his first five Super Bowls, had also shown plenty of creativity, but he said he was uncomfortable with the word *genius*. He said it all boiled down to the players — and maybe he was right.

Super Bowl Sunday was cool and misty, with many fans enjoying their pregame meals in campers parked in the eucalyptus groves at the edge of the handsome campus stadium. It was rare for the highly commercial Super Bowl to have such a collegiate atmosphere.

With 84,059 fans stacked into the old stadium, the Dolphins scored first on a 37-yard field goal by Uwe von Schamann. But the 49ers came right back. Montana completed a 33-yard touchdown play to Carl Monroe, who caught the ball on the 15, broke a tackle, and scored.

Miami went ahead again late in the first quarter when Marino moved the team 70 yards in six plays, scoring on a two-yard pass to Dan Johnson, his tight end. After that, the 49ers' defensive coach, George Seifert, switched from a three-man line to a four-man line, using six defensive backs in most situations. This put more pressure on Marino as the game went on.

Meanwhile, Montana was testing the Dolphins' aging Killer Bee defense. He rolled out, reversed his field, scrambled, and directed three straight scoring drives. Two ended with touchdown passes to Roger Craig, and one with Montana running for a six-yard touchdown. When Von Schamann kicked a 31-yard field goal with 12 seconds remaining in the first half, the 49ers led, 28–13.

There was a moment of terror for the 49ers in the closing seconds of the half as the Dolphins kicked off. The ball went to Guy McIntyre, a reserve guard, who had distinguished himself during the season by acting as a blocking back on a few short-yardage plays. (Walsh had used McIntyre to block against Mike Ditka's Chicago Bears, a move that would lead to the creation of William [Refrigerator] Perry a year later.)

All during Super Bowl week, reporters had asked McIntyre if he had any ambitions to carry the ball. Now, on the kickoff, McIntyre had his hands on the ball — and he did try to run, rather than down the football. Joe Carter of the Dolphins hit him and he fumbled to Jim Jensen of the Dolphins. Von Schamann then kicked a 30-yard field goal to make the score 28–16 at halftime.

The Dolphins' Marino had come from 12 points behind before, but not with Dwaine Board, Fred Dean, Gary Johnson, and Manu Tuiasosopo coming at him from all angles. He was sacked once on his first possession of the second half and twice on the second possession.

Montana was running the Dolphins' defenders into the ground. He set up a 17-yard field goal by

Ray Wersching at 4:48 of the third quarter, and he threw a 16-yard scoring pass to Craig at 8:42. That touchdown by Craig made him the only player ever to score three touchdowns in a Super Bowl.

The Dolphins didn't score again as the 49ers won, 38–16, although Marino made the 49ers' secondary run for their money. He completed 29 of 50 passes, both Super Bowl records, for 318 yards, and was intercepted twice.

Montana gained more yardage, 331, and he completed 24 of 35 passes with no interceptions. But the difference was in his feet. His five rushes gained a total of 59 yards to make him the game's most valuable player.

"A quick quarterback is a necessity in this day and age," Walsh said the next day. But he quickly added, "We have to remind ourselves that yesterday we were considering Marino the greatest passer of all time. He hasn't changed that much, so he didn't have to be mobile. Next year it could be completely reversed."

The happiest man in the 49ers' locker room may have been Guy McIntyre, the reserve guard who had fumbled the ball that led to a field goal. He had spent the second half praying that the three points would not decide the game.

"You envision a lot of things before the Super Bowl," McIntyre said later. "You dream of fumbling the ball and costing the team the game, or getting up when you're not supposed to. But you also dream of picking up the ball and running for a touchdown."

McIntyre's dreams happened to come true, but for Roger Craig and Joe Montana. It was a game for fleet feet and nimble hands, but not necessarily those of Guy McIntyre.

Sweetness and the Refrigerator

As the 1985 season began, the Chicago Bears already possessed the leading runner in pro football history. His name was Walter Payton; his teammates called him "Sweetness" because of his high-pitched voice; and he had already gained 13,909 yards, breaking Jim Brown's career record.

Payton would remain the Bears' *best* runner in 1985, but there were times when he was not necessarily their most publicized runner. That honor, at least for a few giddy months, fell to a rather large young man named William Perry, who wore No. 72 on his back, the number of a tackle.

Perry was a rookie from Clemson University who had been drafted because of his speed as well as his size. Sometimes his size was a problem, however. The Bears wanted him to weigh around 300 pounds; but after putting away a couple of meals of ribs, he might reach 350 pounds. Somebody back home in South Carolina had taken one look at him and dubbed him "The Refrigerator."

The Bears' coaching staff had differing opinions about William Perry. Coach Mike Ditka was intrigued by him, but defensive coach Buddy Ryan wasn't even sure Perry belonged in the league. Ryan and Ditka often disagreed; that's the way things went with the rough, tough Monsters of the Midway.

The Bears, one of the most celebrated franchises in the league, date back to the Decatur Staleys, under George Halas in 1921. Halas was a rugged man who had been a two-way player in the old days, as well as coach, general manager, and, of course, owner.

Over the years, the Bears had many great players, including Bronco Nagurski, Sid Luckman, Bulldog Turner, Dick Butkus, Gayle Sayers, and Walter Payton. One of the favorite players of George Halas was a rugged tight end named Mike Ditka.

Ditka had been the Bears' tight end the last time they won the NFL title in that pre-Super Bowl year of 1963. Halas had let him go, and Ditka later played for Philadelphia and Dallas, and became an assistant coach under Tom Landry of the Cowboys. The two coaches were opposites; Landry was unemotional and intellectual while Halas dated back to the blood-and-guts era, yet Ditka took the best from both of them.

While he was an assistant with the Cowboys, Ditka studied the master technician, Landry, even to the point of wearing a tie on the sidelines. If it was good enough for the master, it was good enough for him.

In 1982 George Halas gave Ditka his first head-coaching job. The tough old man thought Ditka could restore some of the fire to the faded Monsters in an era of computers. Halas could remember when the old Bears just went out there and hit the other team, sometimes even legally.

Not everybody was convinced Ditka was a genius. One Chicago columnist wrote that it would be "madness" to hire Ditka, who had a reputation as somewhat rough around the edges and perhaps not very bright. Halas predicted that Ditka would reach the Super Bowl in three years. Halas did not live to see his prediction come true, but he was off by only one year. The Bears were 3–6 in the strike-shortened 1982 season but then went 8–8 and 10–6 in the next two years.

Ditka got the team's attention early in his regime, when he started pounding a steel locker in the clubhouse. He dismissed the team and then got himself to a hospital for treatment of a broken hand. Football players, who live in a very physical world, were impressed with that act.

The Bears were also impressed with Jim McMahon for the same reason. McMahon was an energetic quarterback from California who somehow wound up at Brigham Young University, even though he wasn't a Mormon, and had no intention of living up to their code of conduct. The brash quarterback was always on the verge of quitting or being dismissed, but he wound up as Brigham Young's leading passer of all time.

With the Bears, McMahon played the role of a punk-rock quarterback to the hilt. He wore wraparound sunglasses to protect an eye he had damaged as a child, and he delighted in dressing and acting like the bad boy in a rock group; but often it seemed he was doing it for effect, to tease the authorities, to liven things up. But he was also a rugged quarterback who did not mind taking a hit if he could gain another yard or two.

And, of course, the Bears still had Sweetness.

They won their first five games in 1985 behind Sweetness and McMahon and the fine defensive unit put together by Buddy Ryan. Sometimes Ryan did not want to use William Perry, whom he had labeled "a wasted draft choice," and Mike Ditka decided, heck, he could use the big fellow.

In the week before the sixth game, Ditka prepared an offensive play called the Refrigerator Play. It involved young Mr. Perry lining up in the offensive backfield, presumably as a blocking back for Sweetness. But Ditka had deeper plans than that; his next opponent was San Francisco.

A year earlier, in the National Conference championship game, the 49ers' coach, Bill Walsh, the man of a thousand offensive plays, had sent in Guy McIntyre, an offensive guard, as a blocking back. He had called the play the Angus Play, not because McIntyre ran like a runaway steer, but because the players frequented a restaurant of the same name.

The 49ers had drubbed the Bears, 23–0, with McIntyre blocking on two key gains. It is safe to say Mike Ditka did not forget it.

In the 1985 meeting, Ditka sent the Refrigerator into the Bears' backfield — but not only to block. On two different occasions, McMahon handed the ball off to Perry, who lumbered forward for two yards each time. Starting in Chicago and spreading around the country, the fans began to be enthralled with this young man with the gap between his two front teeth.

Refrigerator-mania really hit the following week on the *Monday Night Football* show. Playing in front of a national audience, the Bears used Perry in the backfield on plays near the goal line. On two plays, Refrigerator blocked as Payton plowed into the end zone. But on the third play, Perry carried the ball himself for one yard — and a touchdown.

Now the entire nation was in love with Refrigerator. When they learned that he and his wife, Sherry, had a stove, a sink, and a dishwasher, but no refrigerator as yet in their new house, companies began making offers. A dentist even offered to fix the gap in his teeth.

The Refrigerator did not play on offense during the Bears' eighth straight victory but against Green Bay he made his debut as a wide receiver. Perhaps the Packers didn't think the Bears were serious, but when Perry was uncovered, McMahon tossed him a four-yard scoring pass.

After dieting all the way down to 308 pounds, the rookie also became a regular on the defensive line late in the season. He gained more national attention for his antics on November 11. Lining up as Payton's blocker, he saw Sweetness stopped short of the goal line. He tried to lift Payton up and carry him into the end zone. The officials informed Perry that this maneuver was illegal, and they called a penalty on the Bears.

On December 22, Perry ran 59 yards with a recovered fumble but couldn't quite make it into the end zone. He finished the regular season with five rushes for seven yards and two touchdowns, and his third touchdown on the pass reception. The Bears won 15 games and lost only once, to Miami. People began to realize that George Halas's heirs, the McCaskey family, and Jerry Vainisi, Ditka, and Ryan had put together one of the best squads the league had seen in years.

The Bears had a bit of everything: a good offensive line; an unpredictable leader in McMahon; the reliable Sweetness; and a world-class sprinter, Willie Gault, at wide receiver. On defense they had a linebacker named Mike Singletary who could transform himself from a gentle Bible-reading family man into a raving lunatic in the hours before a football game. They had an Ivy League safety named Gary Fencik who would rather run into people than read Thucydides. And on the outside of an excellent defensive line they had Richard Dent.

Dent looked like a limbo dancer until you remembered he was six-five and 263 pounds. He could run fast, turn quickly, and stay out of the way of blockers. He was also motivated because he thought his salary was too low, and all season he was asking the Bears to rewrite his contract for more money. Some players let money problems destroy their concentration, but not Richard Dent. Once the Bears reached the play-offs, Dent began to convince people that he was one of the best defensive ends in the world.

The Bears scored two shutouts in the play-offs, 21–0 over the New York Giants and 24–0 over the Los Angeles Rams, both in their refrigerator of a home stadium, Soldiers Field.

McMahon gathered more attention in the conference title game. He delighted in wearing soft, sweat-absorbing headbands whenever he was on the field. It just happened that his headband carried the name of an equipment manufacturer, and McMahon would display the name whenever he removed his helmet.

Late in the season, the commissioner of the league, Pete Rozelle, fined McMahon and ordered him not to wear the commercial message on his headband again. Like an obedient young man, McMahon complied. The next game, he came out on the field wearing a new headband. This one had the name "Rozelle" inked across the front, for all the world to see. Suddenly, it became a national preoccupation to wonder what Jim McMahon would wear on his headband. He seemed to enjoy keeping people guessing.

He was the same way in the huddle, doing bizarre things to keep the Bears amused, but he was also not afraid of running with the ball. He and Ditka, birds of a feather, did not always stick together. When asked about McMahon, Ditka would make a sour face and say, "He's different."

In January of 1986, the Bears were ready to reverse an old tradition. It is said that jazz moved up the Mississippi River from New Orleans to Chicago. Now Sweetness and the Refrigerator were about to move down the Mississippi to New Orleans. They had plans to make music, all right. On the artificial turf of the Superdome. In a game called the Super Bowl.

Defying History

The New England Patriots do not have the glorious history of the Chicago Bears. They could not look back and talk about Sid Luckman and Bulldog Turner and past championships. Founded in the American Football League in 1960, the Patriots had never won a league title. In fact, they had won only one of five play-off games, back in 1963.

The Patriots did not have a very solid image with fans in distant corners of the league.

"I think our gypsy image started because we kept moving around," said William H. (Billy) Sullivan, Jr., the 70-year-old founder of the Patriots. "We first played at Boston University field for three years. Then Fenway Park, but the Red Sox were doing well and once we had to have a regular-season game against the Jets in Birmingham because the Red Sox needed the field. Then we played at Boston College, then Harvard."

The Patriots finally found a permanent home in a 60,000-seat stadium in Foxboro, Massachusetts. The stadium was renamed Sullivan Stadium in honor of the family that had founded the franchise.

But even that bit of stability was threatened during the 1984 season because the Sullivan family had put the team on the market. Apparently, Chuck Sullivan, Billy's son and a lawyer and the team's executive vice-president, had lost a lot of money promoting a tour by Michael Jackson in 1984.

The year 1984 was not a good one for the Sullivan empire. The Patriots seemed as far from a Super Bowl as ever. Many of their players wanted to leave the Patriots because they did not like the head coach, Ron Meyer. Formerly the coach at Southern Methodist University, Meyer had rules for every tiny detail, including banning popsicles for the players because they did not fit a professional image, and making the offensive and defensive units ride separate buses, to promote unity.

The Sullivan family, which had owned the Patriots since their inception in Boston, stayed with Meyer until he dropped Rod Rust, the defensive coordinator, in the middle of the 1984 season. Even though the Patriots had a 5–3 record, the Sullivans dropped Meyer and replaced him with Raymond Berry, once a smooth receiver for the Baltimore Colts. They also brought back Rust.

The Patriots finished 1984 with a 9–7 record. Hardly anybody would have picked them as Super Bowl candidates for 1985 — particularly since they came out of the same division as the Miami Dolphins and the New York Jets. Berry made a few changes. He brought in Rod Humenuik to coach the offensive linemen; stressed quickness instead of bulk for the linemen; and imported Les Steckel, a bright young receiving coach who had only lasted part of a season as head coach of the Vikings.

The line included Brian Holloway, a Stanford graduate who started a team study program for players without college degrees; John Hannah, the dependable guard; and Steve Moore, a massive tackle nicknamed "House." They opened holes for Craig James, a former Southern Methodist star. Tony Collins, a back, and Stanley Morgan, a wide receiver, made the most catches.

Berry used Tony Eason, 26, as his quarterback, but the Patriots had only a 2–3 record and were losing to Buffalo when Eason's shoulder was injured on a sack. The new quarterback was veteran Steve Grogan, 33, who rallied the team to beat Buffalo and then won five more games. But in the 12th game a New York Jet lineman fell on Grogan's leg, breaking it, and sending the recovered Eason back to quarterback.

By this time, Berry's offensive plan had been fully learned by all the Patriots' players, and Eason, sitting on the bench, had the benefit of watching the veteran Grogan running the plays. Eason came off the bench to help win three of the final four games, as the Patriots qualified for the play-offs.

Rust had developed the defense into a tough unit, led by Andre Tippett and Steve Nelson, the left linebackers; a strong three-man line; and defensive backs Fred Marion and Raymond Clayborn. They ranked seventh in total defensive statistics, but no one seemed to be paying attention.

The Patriots were about to take on the role of the Western movie hero who walks into a saloon and takes care of all the bullies who have manhandled him over the years. Their "saloon" was called the American Conference.

Their first act of revenge was against the Jets in the conference wild-card game, which was played by the two best teams who had not won division titles. The game was played at the Jets' home in New Jersey, and the Jets had a 7–6 lead late in the first half. But with 1:22 remaining, Eason threw a 36-yard touchdown pass to Stanley Morgan, for the 13–7 halftime lead. The Patriots came out and made a key play in the third period, a 15-yard touchdown by Johnny Rembert with a recovered fumble, and they beat the Jets, 26–14.

The next week the Patriots had to travel to Los Angeles for a date with the Raiders. Holloway said it would be a tough assignment because the Raiders are "like sharks. They're in a frenzy this time of year." But Holloway and his linemates opened enough room for Craig James to gain 104 yards, the most by any running back against the Raiders all year.

The Patriots caught the Raiders in a 20–20 tie when Tony Franklin kicked a 32-yard field goal late in the game. On the ensuing kickoff, the Raiders fumbled and Jim Bowman made his second fumble recovery of the day, this one in the end zone for a touchdown.

The Patriots held on for a 27–20 victory, but the action did not end there. During the game, Patrick J. Sullivan, the 33-year-old general manager and one of the owners of the club, had been standing on the sidelines heckling Howie Long of the Raiders. This kind of behavior is unusual for owners and club officials, who usually leave the aggression to the players on the field.

Long, who grew up in the Boston area and weighs 270 pounds, met the 170-pound Sullivan near the tunnel to the clubhouse immediately after the game. They started by yelling, began shoving, and when Sullivan grabbed Long's face mask, another Raider, Matt Millen, responded by swatting Sullivan with his helmet, raising a welt on his forehead.

"Sometimes we let our emotions hang out," Sullivan said, speaking for his family, but promising to stay out of the action the following week.

After two victories on the road, the Patriots now had a third road game — in the Orange Bowl in Miami, where they had lost 18 straight games to the Dolphins. There was a bit of bad blood between these two teams, dating back to the Patriots' use of a snow plow to clear the field for a game-winning field goal during a snowstorm in 1982.

The proud Dolphins, only a game away from a second straight Super Bowl, took a 7-3 lead in the second quarter. But James gained another 105 yards, Marion and Clayborn intercepted Dan Marino passes, and the Patriots controlled the ball for 39:51 in a stunning 31-14 victory.

The Patriots had just become the first team to win three play-off games on the road and qualify for the Super Bowl. It did not bother them that they had lost to Chicago, 20-7, early in the season. And Billy Sullivan, the proud founding father, suspended all talks of selling the club.

"I don't want any distractions. I want to enjoy what's happening, along with my players," Sullivan said, as the Patriots packed for their week in New Orleans.

Jimbo Goes South

Because of its strong French and Spanish heritage, New Orleans is unlike any other American city: narrow streets with restaurants and shops, exotic metal grillwork on balconies overlooking the street, and streets with names like Chartres and Bourbon and Iberville.

Tourists love to visit New Orleans — "The City That Care Forgot" — and in January of 1986 the old town was rocking with a special breed of tourists: football fans, football officials, and, yes, even football players.

It was not unusual to be standing on a crowded intersection in the French Quarter and see William (Refrigerator) Perry walking by, investigating the wonders of a souvenir shop, or Jim McMahon surrounded by youthful admirers, wearing his wraparound sunglasses and giving everybody the thumbs-up sign.

The Bears and the Patriots arrived in New Orleans on Monday, January 20, after a week of quiet preparation for Super Bowl XX. Now they were in the fishbowl of Super Bowl week, magnified 100 percent by its being held in New Orleans.

In most Super Bowl sites, the team and official headquarters were so spread out that it was impossible to get any feeling of an event until game time. At Super Bowl XVII, the Redskins and Dolphins were so spread out over southern California that one visiting reporter said it was like covering the Benelux nations — Belgium, the Netherlands, and Luxembourg. But not New Orleans. Just outside the doors of the hotels were exciting streets, jammed with fans.

In Super Bowl XV, Philadelphia coach Dick Vermeil had tried to keep the Eagles confined to their rooms to avoid the hubbub of New Orleans. However, the Raiders would not stay in their rooms, taking fines from coach Tom Flores and chalking it up to having a good time. This time, the coaches knew better. Both Mike Ditka and Raymond Berry told their players to be sensible and stay out of trouble.

Most everybody did. Being in the same town for a week gave old friends a chance to meet. For Steve Moore, the powerful young tackle for the Patriots, it was a chance to meet his good friend, Richard Dent, the emerging superstar defensive end of the Bears. They had once lived across the hall from each other in Boyd Hall at Tennessee State University in Nashville, and had become close friends.

The first night the Bears and Patriots were in town, Dent left his hotel door open, just the way he always had at Tennessee State. Sure enough, the huge frame of Steve Moore soon filled the doorway, and they spent a few hours talking about old times. The next night they ate together in a restaurant. When Chicago fans spotted them they said, "Beat those Patriots!" Neither Moore nor Dent informed the fans that Moore was, in fact, a member of the Patriots.

During the day, the teams tried to concentrate on football. Bud Grant, who coached the Minnesota Vikings in four Super Bowls, losing all four times, used to say it was not necessary for teams to arrive a full week before the game.

"With or without computers, you could get everything done if you were allowed to go on Thursday night or Friday," Grant said.

However, the National Football League knows that without pictures on television, without words on radio and stories in newspapers, the Super Bowl is just another football game in front of a large crowd. The league is a master at arranging publicity for its big televised event.

The logistics are worthy of the World War II D-day landing in Normandy, France. When the Super Bowl is spread out, reporters wake up while it is still dark, grope their way to a fleet of buses at the hotel, and sit like invading soldiers as the buses roar down the freeway under a dawn sky, for press-day interviews.

In New Orleans, the reporters could sleep later because everything was located downtown. They would jam into hotel meeting rooms and ask questions of the coach, and then mill into another meeting room, where all the players, wearing their names and numbers, were seated at tables. When one team was exhausted, the mob would surge to another hotel for the other team.

As was expected, Jim McMahon provided most of the excitement. He had suffered a bruise on his buttock in a play-off game, and was not able to run well as the week began. After a long morning of answering repetitive questions about his sore spot, McMahon went out to practice and spotted a news helicopter hovering over the practice field. He could not resist: He lowered his practice pants and gave the photographers a rare "photo opportunity" of his injury! Football's bad boy had done it again.

There was more news from McMahon when Hiroshi Shiriashi arrived. Shiriashi was a trainer for the Japanese national track team, skilled in the ancient oriental practice of acupuncture, treating pain with specially made needles.

There is much debate in medical circles about the value of acupuncture, but Willie Gault, the Bears' sprinter-wide receiver, believed the treatments had helped him win a few races in Japan during his college days, and he brought Shiriashi over to treat Walter Payton, McMahon, and himself. The Bears did not invite Shiriashi on the team plane to New Orleans, so Gault invited Shiriashi to be his guest. But the Bears finally allowed the Japanese trainer to treat his clients — adding another exotic twist to this New Orleans Super Bowl.

Because the Super Bowl was close to the Mississippi Delta country, Walter Payton spent his spare time trying to buy up extra tickets for his friends and relatives from Columbia and Jackson, a few hours to the north along the Pearl River.

In Columbia, Payton's favorite coach from high school, Charles Boston, proudly recalled for visiting reporters how Payton had helped ease integration in Columbia with his winning personality and winning football moves.

As Sunday approached, many fans began clogging the small Moisant Airport in New Orleans, while others arrived by special charter train from Chicago. The restaurants were jammed, with the best ones having been reserved weeks and months before.

What is a Super Bowl party like in New Orleans? Dick Schaap, the author; his wife, Trish; and Ham and Midge Richardson, a former tennis star and a magazine editor, co-hosted a private party at K-Paul's, the famous Cajun restaurant of Paul Prudhomme.

Looking around at the party, Arthur Pincus, the assistant sports editor of *The New York Times*, and his wife, Ellen, a teacher, counted two U.S. Senators, Gary Hart of Colorado and Christopher Dodd of Connecticut; one U.S. Representative, Lindy

Boggs of Louisiana; a former member of the Canadian parliament, John Roberts of Toronto; Jimmy Buffett, the country-music singer; Ed Bradley and Bryant Gumbel of television; three former Green Bay Packers — Willie Davis, Marv Fleming, and Jerry Kramer; Bob Pettit, the legendary basketball star; and Nick Lowery, the kicker for the Kansas City Chiefs. Just a friendly little gathering on a Saturday night in New Orleans.

The next afternoon there would be another gathering in New Orleans. This one would not be so friendly.

SUPER BOWL XX

Chicago Bears 46—
New England Patriots 10
January 26, 1986, at New Orleans

The Roof Caves In

It took Walter Payton 10 seasons to break Jim
Brown's all-time rushing record, and 11 seasons to finally reach the Super Bowl. Shortly after
four P.M. on Super Bowl Sunday, in front of a full
house at the Superdome and a worldwide television audience, Payton finally got to carry the ball
in the biggest game of his career.

Starting from his own 18-yard line after Willie
Gault returned the kickoff, Payton darted to the
left side, faking and stutter-stepping. Then he
lowered his shoulder and took a hard tackle from
Steve Nelson after a seven-yard gain, a typical
Walter Payton play.

It worked so well that the Bears decided to give
the ball to Sweetness again, and he drove toward
right guard only to be hit by Don Blackmon. Suddenly Payton fumbled the ball, and Larry McGrew
recovered on the 19. The game was only 59 seconds old, and already there had been a break.

Tony Eason, the Patriots' quarterback who had

been suffering from the flu, missed three straight passes, and the Patriots settled for Tony Franklin's 36-yard field goal.

Was this the start of an upset? New England fans had every reason to hope so, but the Bears did not let the first score of the game affect them. Some people had worried that Jim McMahon would let all the pregame attention interfere with his game, but McMahon seemed to thrive on excitement. After a week of enjoying the frenzy in the French Quarter, McMahon was wide awake at game time.

After his antics with the "Rozelle" headband during the play-offs, McMahon knew his headband would be under scrutiny by league officials this week. He came out on the field wearing a headband that said, "JDF Cure," praising the work of the Juvenile Diabetes Foundation. (A few weeks later, the JDF would praise McMahon for bringing in $30,000 in donations that day.)

Never would McMahon have a bigger audience. He moved the Bears 59 yards in eight plays before Kevin Butler, who also had been suffering from the flu, kicked a 28-yard field goal to tie the score.

Once again, Eason could not complete a pass, and the Patriots had to punt. The Bears also punted. But on the second play, Richard Dent went roaring around the blockers to sack Eason. The ball squirted loose, and Dan Hampton, known as "Danimal," recovered.

The Bears made a first down and then Payton lost two yards, back to the Patriots' five. Into the game came the Bears' ultimate offensive weapon, none other than Refrigerator Perry. Many people in the audience gasped with surprise to see the burly No. 72 come rumbling onto the field. Many people had thought he was a gimmick, to keep the Bears amused during the midseason blahs, but Coach Ditka was not afraid to use him in the Super Bowl.

Lining up as a running back, Perry took a handoff from McMahon and began moving at his own pace toward the right side. As the Patriots moved toward him, Perry pumped his arm to pass, and then he pumped again. The Patriots and the fans could not help but remember all those funny photographs of Perry tossing the ball in practice. He wouldn't dare throw a pass — would he? Not this time. Perry held the ball as Dennis Owens sacked him for a yard loss, setting an unofficial record for the largest man ever sacked while apparently attempting to pass.

After McMahon missed on a pass, Butler kicked a 24-yard field goal to put the Bears ahead, 6–3. Had both teams gotten over their Super Bowl shakes and made their one early mistake? Hardly. On the first play after the kickoff, Craig James, a dependable runner all season, fumbled while being hit by Dent, and Mike Singletary recovered on the Patriots' 13.

Was this a chance for Sweetness Payton to score his first Super Bowl touchdown? Not with the Patriots expecting Sweetness to run with the ball. McMahon handled off to Matt Suhey, the chunky blocking back, who bulled ahead for two yards. Then Suhey surprised many people by bursting for an 11-yard touchdown that helped the Bears go ahead, 13–3, at the end of the first quarter.

Having posed as a passing threat, Perry performed on defense, smothering James as the Patriots again failed to make a first down. Then McMahon engineered a long 59-yard drive, scoring himself on a romp around left end, behind Tim Wrightman and another active blocker — you guessed it, the Refrigerator. Now the score was 20–3.

Late in the second quarter, Raymond Berry changed quarterbacks, taking out Eason, who had not completed any of his six passes, and sending in the veteran, Steve Grogan.

In the press box, reporters were informed that "Eason has no injury or illness," but anyone could see he had a bad case of Buddy Ryan's defense. Grogan couldn't move the team, either, and the Bears took a 23–3 lead on a 25-yard field goal by Butler.

The second half was more of the same. Grogan couldn't move the Patriots, and although Rich Camarillo punted for 62 yards, the Bears did not mind starting from their own four-yard line. The two acupuncture patients, McMahon and Gault, looked extremely nimble on a 60-yard pass play.

At this point, many Bears' fans and other admirers of Walter Payton were looking for Sweetness to get the call, but he never saw the ball after the Bears reached the 16. Once they reached the one-yard line, McMahon bolted over the middle for a touchdown to put the Bears ahead, 30–3.

In the next four minutes, the Bears would score twice more. Reggie Phillips, a defensive back, who was in the game after Leslie Frazier injured his knee in the opening minutes, picked off a deflected pass for a 28-yard touchdown and a 37–3 lead.

Could things get any worse for the Patriots? Yes, they could. Grogan completed a pass, but the ball was fumbled and recovered by Wilber Marshall. The Bears were so confident that Marshall was able to toss a lateral pass to Otis Wilson before the Patriots made the tackle on the New England 37.

For a while, it seemed that Payton would get his first Super Bowl touchdown, as he ran the ball three times and then had a pass thrown to him. But McMahon's big play was a 27-yard completion to Dennis Gentry on the Patriots' one-yard line.

Was this Payton's chance? Ditka sent in Perry, but instead of being used as a blocker for Payton, Perry heard his own signal being called, and the big rookie followed orders, lumbering in for a Super

Bowl touchdown, the final touch on an incredible rookie season.

Refrigerator Perry had gone from a rookie ignored by his own defensive-unit coach to a respectable defensive lineman who doubled as a Super Bowl offensive force. Every time he did something in the Super Bowl it was worth a new commercial for him.

The rest of the Bears were all having a magnificent game, too. They did give up a touchdown on a pass from Grogan to Irving Fryar. That made the score 44–10. The final two points of the game came on a safety by Henry Waechter, who tackled Grogan in the end zone.

When the game came to a merciful end, Pete Rozelle presented the Super Bowl Trophy to Edward McCaskey and Michael McCaskey, two members of the Halas family who had led the Bears to the title.

"The Monsters of the Midway have really returned," Rozelle said. "It is the biggest win in Super Bowl history — and only one loss in an 18–1 season."

Ditka, the gruff head coach who had played tight end on the Bears' last championship team in 1963, recalled that George Halas's birthday would have been on February 2. Ditka added: "This is a fitting tribute to Mr. Halas. I always think of George Halas. Because of him, I'm here."

A few minutes after the game, it was announced that Richard Dent, the defensive end who had been trying to renegotiate his contract all season, was voted the outstanding player in the Super Bowl. His monster of a game would cost somebody some money; the Bears were all saying privately that the Bears' management absolutely had to pay Dent enough money to keep him in the Bears' uniform for years to come.

The final score of 46–10 was not the only indication of the Bears' superiority. They outgained the Patriots, 408 yards to 123, and they held the ball for 39:15, compared to the 20:45 of the Patriots. McMahon finished with 12 of 20 passes for 256 yards. Walter Payton was the leading ground-gainer with 61 yards in 22 carries — hardly one of his better days.

While most of the Bears celebrated noisily in the crowded locker room, pouring champagne on each other and mugging for the television cameras, Payton did not seem as enthusiastic as his teammates. It took a long time before he showered and dressed and then appeared in the press-interview room.

Somebody asked Payton if he was surprised that he did not get the ball close to the goal line.

"Yeah," he replied.

Was Payton disappointed?

"Yeah."

But he quickly added, "When they're keying on you, you can't mind. I don't mind being the rabbit," a sports term for the decoy or runner who sets the early pace in a track race.

Some of the Bears professed that they did not realize Payton had not scored. Steve Fuller, the second-string quarterback, admitted he had tried calling Payton's signal late in the game but that Payton "didn't like it a bit," feeling that a touchdown at that time might have seemed like charity.

"He's the heart and soul of this organization," Fuller said. "I don't think scoring a touchdown would have made any difference."

The "heart and soul" looked tired as he told reporters: "You've known me for 11 years. I'm happy but I don't know how to express it, so I just sit back and enjoy it."

Payton had waited 11 seasons for this moment, and he was not going to let the lack of a touchdown ruin it for him. Most players never experience what Payton was quietly enjoying at that moment: the feeling that his team was the Super Bowl champion, and nobody could ever take that away from him.

Records

Scoring Summaries

SUPER BOWL I

Green Bay 35, Kansas City 10
January 15, 1967 at Los Angeles

Kansas City	......	0	10	0	0 — 10
Green Bay	....	7	7	14	7 — 35

GB—McGee 37 pass from Starr
    (Chandler kick)
KC—McClinton 7 pass from Dawson
    (Mercer kick)
GB—Taylor 14 run (Chandler kick)
KC—FG Mercer 31
GB—Pitts 5 run (Chandler kick)
GB—McGee 13 pass from Starr
    (Chandler kick)
GB—Pitts 1 run (Chandler kick)
Attendance—61,946

TEAM STATISTICS	KC	GB
First downs	17	21
Rushing	4	10
Passing	12	11
By penalty	1	0
Total yardage	239	358
Net rushing yardage	72	130
Net passing yardage	167	228
Passes att.-comp.		
-had int.	32-17-1	24-16-1

Rushing
Kansas City—Dawson, 3 for 24; Garrett, 6 for 17; McClinton, 6 for 16; Beathard, 1 for 14; Coan, 3 for 1.
Green Bay—J. Taylor, 16 for 53, 1 TD; Pitts, 11 for 45, 2 TDs; D. Anderson, 4 for 30; Grabowski, 2 for 2.
Passing
Kansas City—Dawson, 16 of 27 for 211, 1 TD, 1 int.; Beathard, 1 of 5 for 17.
Green Bay—Starr, 16 of 23 for 250, 2 TDs, 1 int.; Bratkowski, 0 of 1.
Receiving
Kansas City—Burford, 4 for 67; O. Taylor, 4 for 57; Garrett, 3 for 28; McClinton, 2 for 34, 1 TD; Arbanas, 2 for 30; Carolan, 1 for 7; Coan, 1 for 5.
Green Bay—McGee, 7 for 138, 2 TDs; Dale, 4 for 59; Pitts, 2 for 32; Fleming, 2 for 22; J. Taylor, 1 for −1.

SUPER BOWL II

Green Bay 33, Oakland 14
January 14, 1968 at Miami

Green Bay	....	3	13	10	7 — 33
Oakland	....	0	7	0	7 — 14

GB —FG Chandler 39
GB —FG Chandler 20
GB —Dowler 62 pass from Starr
    (Chandler kick)
Oak—Miller 23 pass from Lamonica
    (Blanda kick)
GB —FG Chandler 43
GB —Anderson 2 run (Chandler kick)
GB —FG Chandler 31
GB —Adderley 60 interception return
    (Chandler kick)
Oak—Miller 23 pass from Lamonica
    (Blanda kick)
Attendance—75,546

TEAM STATISTICS	GB	OAK
First downs	19	16
Rushing	11	5
Passing	7	10
By penalty	1	1
Total yardage	322	293
Net rushing yardage	160	107
Net passing yardage	162	186
Passes att.-comp.		
-had int.	24-13-0	34-15-1

Rushing
Green Bay—Wilson, 17 for 62; Anderson, 14 for 48; 1 TD; Williams, 8 for 36; Starr, 1 for 14; Mercein, 1 for 0.
Oakland—Dixon, 12 for 54; Todd, 2 for 37; Banaszak, 6 for 16.
Passing
Green Bay—Starr, 13 of 24 for 202, 1 TD.
Oakland—Lamonica, 15 of 34 for 208, 2 TDs, 1 int.
Receiving
Green Bay—Dale, 4 for 43; Fleming, 4 for 35; Anderson, 2 for 18; Dowler, 2 for 71, 1 TD; McGee, 1 for 35.
Oakland—Miller, 5 for 84, 2 TDs; Banaszak, 4 for 69; Cannon, 2 for 25; Biletnikoff, 2 for 10; Wells, 1 for 17; Dixon, 1 for 3.

SUPER BOWL III

N.Y. Jets 16, Baltimore 7
January 12, 1969 at Miami

New York Jets...   0   7   6   3 — 16
Baltimore..........   0   0   0   7 — 7

NYJ—Snell 4 run (Turner kick)
NYJ—FG Turner 32
NYJ—FG Turner 30
NYJ—FG Turner 9
Balt—Hill 1 run (Michaels kick)
Attendance—75,389

TEAM STATISTICS	NYJ	BALT
First downs	21	18
Rushing	10	7
Passing	10	9
By penalty	1	2
Total yardage	337	324
Net rushing yardage	142	143
Net passing yardage	195	181
Passes att.-comp.		
-had int.	29-17-0	41-17-4

Rushing
New York Jets—Snell, 30 for 121, 1 TD; Boozer, 10 for 19; Mathis, 3 for 2.
Baltimore—Matte, 11 for 116; Hill, 9 for 29, 1 TD; Unitas, 1 for 0; Morrall, 2 for −2.

Passing
New York Jets—Namath, 17 of 28 for 206; Parilli, 0 of 1.
Baltimore—Morrall, 6 of 17 for 71, 3 int.; Unitas, 11 of 24 for 110, 1 int.

Receiving
New York Jets—Sauer, 8 for 133; Snell, 4 for 40; Mathis, 3 for 20; Lammons, 2 for 13.
Baltimore—Richardson, 6 for 58; Orr, 3 for 42; Mackey, 3 for 35; Matte, 2 for 30; Hill, 2 for 1; Mitchell, 1 for 15.

SUPER BOWL IV

Kansas City 23, Minnesota 7
January 11, 1970 at New Orleans

Minnesota.........   0   0   7   0 — 7
Kansas City   3   13   7   0 — 23

KC —FG Stenerud 48
KC —FG Stenerud 32
KC —FG Stenerud 25
KC —Garrett 5 run (Stenerud kick)
Minn—Osborn 4 run (Cox kick)
KC —(Taylor 46 pass from Dawson (Stenerud kick)
Attendance—80,562

TEAM STATISTICS	MINN	KC
First downs	13	18
Rushing	2	8
Passing	10	7
By penalty	1	3
Total yardage	239	273
Net rushing yardage	67	151
Net passing yardage	172	122
Passes att.-comp.		
-had int.	28-17-3	17-12-1

Rushing
Minnesota—Brown, 6 for 26; Reed, 4 for 17; Osborn, 7 for 15, 1 TD; Kapp, 2 for 9.
Kansas City—Garrett, 11 for 39, 1 TD; Pitts, 3 for 37; Hayes, 8 for 31; McVea, 12 for 26; Dawson, 3 for 11; Holmes, 5 for 7.

Passing
Minnesota—Kapp, 16 of 25 for 183, 2 int.; Cuozzo, 1 of 3 for 16, 1 int.
Kansas City—Dawson, 12 of 17 for 142, 1 TD, 1 int.

Receiving
Minnesota—Henderson, 7 for 111; Brown, 3 for 11; Beasley, 2 for 41; Reed, 2 for 16; Osborn, 2 for 11; Washington, 1 for 9.
Kansas City—Taylor, 6 for 81, 1 TD; Pitts, 3 for 33; Garrett, 2 for 25; Hayes, 1 for 3.

SUPER BOWL V

Baltimore 16, Dallas 13
January 17, 1971 at Miami

Baltimore	0	6	0	10 —	16
Dallas	3	10	0	0 —	13

Dall—FG Clark 14
Dall—FG Clark 30
Balt—Mackey 75 pass from Unitas (kick blocked)
Dall—Thomas 7 pass from Morton (Clark kick)
Balt—Nowatzke 2 run (O'Brien kick)
Balt—FG O'Brien 32
Attendance—79,204

TEAM STATISTICS

	BALT	DALL
First downs	14	10
Rushing	4	4
Passing	6	5
By penalty	4	1
Total yardage	329	215
Net rushing yardage	69	102
Net passing yardage	260	113
Passes att.-comp.		
-had int.	25-11-3	26-12-3

Rushing
Baltimore—Nowatzke, 10 for 33, 1 TD; Bulaich, 18 for 28; Unitas, 1 for 4; Havrilak, 1 for 3; Morrall, 1 for 1.
Dallas—Garrison, 12 for 65; Thomas, 18 for 35; Morton, 1 for 2.

Passing
Baltimore—Unitas, 3 of 9 for 88, 1 TD, 2 int.; Morrall, 7 of 15 for 147, 1 int.; Havrilak, 1 of 1 for 25.
Dallas—Morton, 12 of 26 for 127, 1 TD, 3 int.

Receiving
Baltimore—Jefferson, 3 for 52; Mackey, 2 for 80, 1 TD; Hinton, 2 for 51; Havrilak, 2 for 27; Nowatzke, 1 for 45; Bulaich, 1 for 5.
Dallas—Reeves, 5 for 46; Thomas, 4 for 21, 1 TD; Garrison, 2 for 19; Hayes, 1 for 41.

SUPER BOWL VI

Dallas 24, Miami 3
January 16, 1972 at New Orleans

Dallas	3	7	7	7 —	24
Miami	0	3	0	0 —	3

Dall—FG Clark 9
Dall—Alworth 7 pass from Staubach (Clark kick)
Mia—FG Yepremian 31
Dall—D. Thomas 3 run (Clark kick)
Dall—Ditka 7 pass from Staubach (Clark kick)
Attendance—81,023

TEAM STATISTICS

	DALL	MIA
First downs	23	10
Rushing	15	3
Passing	8	7
By penalty	0	0
Total yardage	352	185
Net rushing yardage	252	80
Net passing yardage	100	105
Passes att.-comp.		
-had int.	19-12-0	23-12-1

Rushing
Dallas—D. Thomas, 19 for 95, 1 TD; Garrison, 14 for 74; Hill, 7 for 25; Staubach, 5 for 18; Ditka, 1 for 17; Hayes, 1 for 16; Reeves, 1 for 7.
Miami—Csonka, 9 for 40; Kiick, 10 for 40; Griese, 1 for 0.

Passing
Dallas—Staubach, 12 of 19 for 119, 2 TDs.
Miami—Griese, 12 of 23 for 134, 1 int.

Receiving
Dallas—D. Thomas, 3 for 17; Alworth, 2 for 28, 1 TD; Ditka, 2 for 28, 1 TD; Hayes, 2 for 23; Garrison, 2 for 11; Hill, 1 for 12.
Miami—Warfield, 4 for 39; Kiick, 3 for 21; Csonka, 2 for 18; Fleming, 1 for 27; Twilley, 1 for 20; Mandich, 1 for 9.

SUPER BOWL VII

Miami 14, Washington 7
January 14, 1973 at Los Angeles

Miami	7	7	0	0	— 14
Washington	0	0	0	7	— 7

Mia —Twilley 28 pass from Griese
    (Yepremian kick)
Mia —Kiick 1 run (Yepremian kick)
Wash—Bass 49 fumble return
    (Knight kick)
Attendance—90,182

TEAM STATISTICS	MIA	WASH
First downs	12	16
Rushing	7	9
Passing	5	7
By penalty	0	0
Total yardage	253	228
Net rushing yardage	184	141
Net passing yardage	69	87
Passes att.-comp.		
-had int.	11-8-1	28-14-3

Rushing
Miami—Csonka, 15 for 112; Kiick, 12 for 38, 1 TD; Morris, 10 for 34.
Washington—Brown, 22 for 72; Harraway, 10 for 37; Kilmer, 2 for 18; C. Taylor, 1 for 8; Smith, 1 for 6.

Passing
Miami—Griese, 8 of 11 for 88, 1 TD, 1 int.
Washington—Kilmer, 14 of 28 for 104, 3 int.

Receiving
Miami—Warfield, 3 for 36; Kiick, 2 for 6; Twilley, 1 for 28, 1 TD; Mandich, 1 for 19; Csonka, 1 for −1.
Washington—Jefferson, 5 for 50; Brown, 5 for 26; C. Taylor, 2 for 20; Smith, 1 for 11; Harraway, 1 for −3.

SUPER BOWL VIII

Miami 24, Minnesota 7
January 13, 1974 at Houston

Minnesota	0	0	0	7	— 7
Miami	14	3	7	0	— 24

Mia —Csonka 5 run
    (Yepremian kick)
Mia —Kiick 1 run (Yepremian kick)
Mia —FG Yepremian 28
Mia —Csonka 2 run
    (Yepremian kick)
Minn—Tarkenton 4 run (Cox kick)
Attendance—71,882

TEAM STATISTICS	MINN	MIA
First downs	14	21
Rushing	5	13
Passing	8	4
By penalty	1	4
Total yardage	238	259
Net rushing yardage	72	196
Net passing yardage	166	63
Passes att.-comp.		
-had int.	28-18-1	7-6-0

Rushing
Minnesota—Reed, 11 for 32; Foreman, 7 for 18; Tarkenton; 4 for 17, 1 TD; Marinaro, 1 for 3; B. Brown, 1 for 6.
Miami—Csonka, 33 for 145, 2 TDs; Morris, 11 for 34; Kiick, 7 for 10, 1 TD; Griese, 2 for 7.

Passing
Minnesota—Tarkenton, 18 of 28 for 182, 1 int.
Miami—Griese, 6 of 7 for 73.

Receiving
Minnesota—Foreman, 5 for 27; Gilliam, 4 for 44, Voigt, 3 for 46; Marinaro, 2 for 39; B. Brown, 1 for 9; Kingsriter, 1 for 9; Lash, 1 for 9; Reed, 1 for −1.
Miami—Warfield, 2 for 33; Mandich, 2 for 21; Briscoe, 2 for 19.

SUPER BOWL IX

Pittsburgh 16, Minnesota 6
January 12, 1975 at New Orleans

Pittsburgh	....	0	2	7	7 — 16
Minnesota	....	0	0	0	6 — 6

Pitt —Safety, White downed
    Tarkenton in end zone
Pitt —Harris 9 run (Gerela kick)
Minn—T. Brown recovered blocked
    punt in end zone (kick failed)
Pitt —L. Brown 4 pass from
    Bradshaw (Gerela kick)
Attendance—80,997

TEAM STATISTICS

	PITT	MINN
First downs	17	9
Rushing	11	2
Passing	5	5
By penalty	1	2
Total yardage	333	119
Net rushing yardage	249	17
Net passing yardage	84	102
Passes att.-comp.		
-had int.	14-9-0	26-11-3

Rushing
Pittsburgh—Harris, 34 for 158, 1 TD;
Bleier, 17 for 65; Bradshaw, 5 for 33;
Swann, 1 for −7.
Minnesota—Foreman, 12 for 18; Tarkenton, 1 for 0; Osborn, 8 for −1.

Passing
Pittsburgh—Bradshaw, 9 of 14 for 96,
1 TD.
Minnesota—Tarkenton, 11 of 26 for 102,
3 int.

Receiving
Pittsburgh—Brown, 3 for 49, 1 TD;
Stallworth, 3 for 24; Bleier, 2 for 11;
Lewis, 1 for 12.
Minnesota—Foreman, 5 for 50; Voigt,
2 for 31; Osborn, 2 for 7; Gilliam, 1 for
16; Reed, 1 for −2.

SUPER BOWL X

Pittsburgh 21, Dallas 17
January 18, 1976 at Miami

Dallas	....	7	3	0	7 — 17
Pittsburgh	....	7	0	0	14 — 21

Dall—D. Pearson 29 pass from
    Staubach (Fritsch kick)
Pitt—Grossman 7 pass from Bradshaw
    (Gerela kick)
Dall—FG Fritsch 36
Pitt—Safety, Harrison blocked
    Hoopes's punt through end zone.
Pitt—FG Gerela 36
Pitt—FG Gerela 18
Pitt—Swann 64 pass from Bradshaw
    (kick failed)
Dall—P. Howard 34 pass from
    Staubach (Fritsch kick)
Attendance—80,187

TEAM STATISTICS

	DALL	PITT
First downs	14	13
Rushing	6	7
Passing	8	6
By penalty	0	0
Total yardage	270	339
Net rushing yardage	108	149
Net passing yardage	162	190
Passes att.-comp.		
-had int.	24-15-3	19-9-0

Rushing
Dallas—Newhouse, 16 for 56; Staubach, 5 for 22; Dennison, 5 for 16; P.
Pearson, 5 for 14.
Pittsburgh—Harris, 27 for 82; Bleier,
15 for 51; Bradshaw, 4 for 16.

Passing
Dallas—Staubach, 15 of 24 for 204, 2
TDs, 3 int.
Pittsburgh—Bradshaw, 9 of 19 for 209,
2 TDs.

Receiving
Dallas—P. Pearson, 5 for 53; Young,
3 for 31; D. Pearson, 2 for 59, 1 TD;
Newhouse, 2 for 12; P. Howard, 1 for
34, 1 TD; Fugett, 1 for 9; Dennison,
1 for 6.
Pittsburgh—Swann, 4 for 161, 1 TD;
Stallworth, 2 for 8; Harris, 1 for 26;
Grossman, 1 for 7; L. Brown, 1 for 7.

SUPER BOWL XI

Oakland 32, Minnesota 14
January 9, 1977 at Pasadena

Oakland	0	16	3	13 —	32
Minnesota	0	0	7	7 —	14

Oak —FG Mann 24
Oak —Casper 1 pass from Stabler (Mann kick)
Oak —Banaszak 1 run (kick failed)
Oak —FG Mann 40
Minn —White 8 pass from Tarkenton (Cox kick)
Oak —Banaszak 2 run (Mann kick)
Oak —Brown 75 interception return (kick failed)
Minn —Voigt 13 pass from Lee (Cox kick)
Attendance—103,438

TEAM STATISTICS	OAK	MINN
First downs	21	20
Rushing	13	2
Passing	8	15
By penalty	0	3
Total yardage	429	353
Net rushing yardage	266	71
Net passing yardage	163	282
Passes att.-comp.		
-had int.	19-12-0	44-24-2

Rushing
Oakland—Davis, 16 for 137; van Eeghen, 18 for 73; Garrett, 4 for 19; Banaszak, 10 for 19, 2 TDs; Ginn, 2 for 9; Roe, 2 for 9.
Minnesota—Foreman, 17 for 44; McClanahan, 3 for 3; Miller, 2 for 4; Lee, 1 for 4; S. White, 1 for 7; Johnson, 2 for 9.

Passing
Oakland—Stabler, 12 for 19 for 180, 1 TD.
Minnesota—Tarkenton, 17 of 35 for 205, 1 TD, 2 int.; Lee, 7 of 9 for 81, 1 TD.

Receiving
Oakland—Biletnikoff, 4 for 79; Casper, 4 for 70, 1 TD; Garrett, 1 for 11; Branch, 3 for 20.
Minnesota—S. White, 5 for 77, 1 TD; Foreman, 5 for 62; Voigt, 4 for 49, 1 TD; Miller, 4 for 19; Rashad, 3 for 53; Johnson, 3 for 26.

SUPER BOWL XII

Dallas 27, Denver 10
January 15, 1978 at New Orleans

Dallas	10	3	7	7 —	27
Denver	0	0	10	0 —	10

Dall—Dorsett 3 run (Herrera kick)
Dall—FG Herrera 35
Dall—FG Herrera 43
Den—FG Turner 47
Dall—Johnson 45 pass from Staubach (Herrera kick)
Den—Lytle 1 run (Turner kick)
Dall—Richards 29 pass from Newhouse (Herrera kick)
Attendance—75,583

TEAM STATISTICS	DALL	DEN
First downs	17	11
Rushing	8	8
Passing	8	1
By penalty	1	2
Total yardage	325	156
Net rushing yardage	143	121
Net passing yardage	182	35
Passes att.-comp.		
-had int.	28-19-0	25-8-4

Rushing
Dallas—Dorsett, 15 for 66, 1 TD; Newhouse, 14 for 55; White, 1 for 13; P. Pearson, 3 for 11; Staubach, 3 for 6; Laidlaw, 1 for 1; Johnson, 1 for −9.
Denver—Lytle, 10 for 35, 1 TD; Armstrong, 7 for 27; Weese, 3 for 26; Jensen, 1 for 16; Keyworth, 5 for 9; Perrin, 3 for 8.

Passing
Dallas—Staubach, 17 of 25 for 183, 1 TD; White, 1 of 2 for 5; Newhouse, 1 of 1 for 29, 1 TD.
Denver—Morton, 4 of 15 for 39, 4 int.; Weese, 4 of 10 for 22.

Receiving
Dallas—P. Pearson, 5 for 37; DuPree, 4 for 66; Newhouse, 3 for −1; Johnson, 2 for 53, 1 TD; Richards, 2 for 38, 1 TD; Dorsett, 2 for 11; D. Pearson, 1 for 13.
Denver—Dolbin, 2 for 24; Odoms, 2 for 9; Moses, 1 for 21; Upchurch, 1 for 9; Jensen, 1 for 5; Perrin, 1 for −7.

SUPER BOWL XIII

Pittsburgh 35, Dallas 31
January 21, 1979 at Miami

Pittsburgh	....	7	14	0	14	— 35
Dallas	....	7	7	3	14	— 31

Pitt —Stallworth 28 pass from
    Bradshaw (Gerela kick)
Dall —Hill 39 pass from Staubach
    (Septien kick)
Dall —Hegman 37 fumble recovery
    return (Septien kick)
Pitt —Stallworth 75 pass from
    Bradshaw (Gerela kick)
Pitt —Bleier 7 pass from Bradshaw
    (Gerela kick)
Dall —FG Septien 27
Pitt —Harris 22 run (Gerela kick)
Pitt —Swann 18 pass from Bradshaw
    (Gerela kick)
Dall —DuPree 7 pass from Staubach
    (Septien kick)
Dall —B. Johnson 4 pass from
    Staubach (Septien kick)
Attendance—79,484

TEAM STATISTICS

	PITT	DALL
First downs	19	20
Rushing	2	6
Passing	15	13
By penalty	2	1
Total yardage	357	330
Net rushing yardage	66	154
Net passing yardage	291	176
Passes att.-comp.		
-had int.	30-17-1	30-17-1

Rushing

Pittsburgh—Harris, 20 for 68, 1 TD;
Bleier, 2 for 3; Bradshaw, 1 for −5.
Dallas—Dorsett, 16 for 96; Staubach,
4 for 37; Laidlaw, 3 for 12; P. Pearson,
1 for 6; Newhouse, 8 for 3.

Passing

Pittsburgh—Bradshaw, 17 of 30 for 318,
4 TDs, 1 int.
Dallas—Staubach, 17 of 30 for 228, 3
TDs, 1 int.

Receiving

Pittsburgh—Swann, 7 for 124, 1 TD;
Stallworth, 3 for 115, 2 TDs; Grossman, 3 for 29; Bell, 2 for 21; Harris,
1 for 22; Bleier, 1 for 7, 1 TD.
Dallas—Dorsett, 5 for 44; D. Pearson,
4 for 73; Hill, 2 for 49, 1 TD; Johnson,
2 for 30, 1 TD; DuPree, 2 for 17, 1 TD;
P. Pearson, 2 for 15.

SUPER BOWL XIV

Pittsburgh 31, Los Angeles 19
January 20, 1980 at Pasadena

Los Angeles	......	7	6	6	0	— 19
Pittsburgh	....	3	7	7	14	— 31

Pitt—FG Bahr 41
LA —Bryant 1 run (Corral kick)
Pitt—Harris 1 run (Bahr kick)
LA —FG Corral 31
LA —FG Corral 45
Pitt—Swann 47 pass from Bradshaw
    (Bahr kick)
LA —Smith 24 pass from McCutcheon
    (kick failed)
Pitt—Stallworth 73 pass from
    Bradshaw (Bahr kick)
Pitt—Harris 1 run (Bahr kick)
Attendance—103,985

TEAM STATISTICS

	LA	PITT
First downs	16	19
Rushing	6	8
Passing	9	10
By penalty	1	1
Total yardage	301	393
Net rushing yardage	107	84
Net passing yardage	194	309
Passes att.-comp.		
-had int.	26-16-1	21-14-3

Rushing

Los Angeles—Tyler, 17 for 60; Bryant,
6 for 30, 1 TD; McCutcheon, 5 for 10;
Ferragamo, 1 for 7.
Pittsburgh—Harris, 20 for 46, 2 TDs;
Bleier, 10 for 25; Bradshaw, 3 for 9;
Thornton, 4 for 4.

Passing

Los Angeles—Ferragamo, 15 of 25 for
212, 1 int.; McCutcheon, 1 of 1 for 24,
1 TD.
Pittsburgh—Bradshaw, 14 of 21 for 309,
2 TDs, 3 int.

Receiving

Los Angeles—Waddy, 3 for 75; Bryant,
3 for 21; Tyler, 3 for 20; Dennard, 2
for 32; Nelson, 2 for 20; D. Hill, 1 for
28; Smith, 1 for 24, 1 TD; McCutcheon,
1 for 16.
Pittsburgh—Swann, 5 for 79, 1 TD;
Stallworth, 3 for 121, 1 TD; Harris, 3
for 66; Cunningham, 2 for 21; Thornton,
1 for 22.

141

SUPER BOWL XV

Oakland 27, Philadelphia 10
Janaury 25, 1981 at New Orleans

Oakland	14	0	10	3 — 27
Philadelphia	0	3	0	7 — 10

Oak—Branch 2 pass from Plunkett
(Bahr kick)
Oak—King 80 pass from Plunkett
(Bahr kick)
Phil—FG Franklin 30
Oak—Branch 29 pass from Plunkett
(Bahr kick)
Oak—FG Bahr 46
Phil—Krepfle 8 pass from Jaworski
(Franklin kick)
Oak—FG Bahr 35
Attendance—76,135

TEAM STATISTICS	OAK	PHIL
First downs	17	19
Rushing	6	3
Passing	10	14
By penalty	1	2
Total yardage	377	360
Net rushing yardage	117	69
Net passing yardage	260	291
Passes att.-comp.		
-had int.	21-13-0	38-18-3

Rushing
Oakland—van Eeghen, 19 for 80; King,
6 for 18; Jensen, 3 for 12; Plunkett, 3
for 9; Whittington, 3 for -2.
Philadelphia—Montgomery, 16 for 44;
Harris, 7 for 14; Giammona, 1 for 7;
Harrington, 1 for 4; Jaworski, 1 for 0.

Passing
Oakland—Plunkett, 13 of 21 for 261,
3 TD.
Phila.—Jaworski, 18 of 38 for 291, 1
TD, 3 int.

Receiving
Oakland—Branch, 5 for 67, 2 TD;
Chandler, 4 for 77; King, 2 for 93, 1
TD; Chester, 2 for 24.
Philadelphia—Montgomery, 6 for 91;
Carmichael, 5 for 83; Smith, 2 for 59;
Krepfle, 2 for 16, 1 TD; Spagnola,
1 for 22; Parker, 1 for 19; Harris, 1
for 1.

SUPER BOWL XVI

San Francisco 26, Cincinnati 21
January 24, 1982 at Pontiac,
Michigan

San Francisco	7	13	0	6 — 26
Cincinnati	0	0	7	14 — 21

SF —Montana 1 run (Wersching kick)
SF —Cooper 11 pass from Montana
(Wersching kick)
SF —FG Wersching 22
SF —FG Wersching 26
Cin—Anderson 5 run (Breech kick)
Cin—Ross 4 pass from Anderson
(Breech kick)
SF —FG Wersching 40
SF —FG Wersching 23
Cin—Ross 3 pass from Anderson
(Breech kick)
Attendance—81,270

TEAM STATISTICS	SF	CIN
First downs	20	24
Rushing	9	7
Passing	9	13
By penalty	2	4
Total yardage	275	356
Net rushing yardage	127	72
Net passing yardage	148	284
Passes att.-comp.		
-had int.	22-14-0	34-25-2

Rushing
San Francisco—Patton, 17 for 55;
Cooper, 9 for 34; Montana, 6 for 18, 1
TD; Ring, 5 for 17; J. Davis, 2 for 5;
Clark, 1 for −2.
Cincinnati—Johnson, 14 for 36; Alex-
ander, 5 for 17; Anderson, 4 for 15; A.
Griffin, 1 for 4.

Passing
San Francisco—Montana, 14 of 22 for
157, 1 TD.
Cincinnati—Anderson, 25 of 34 for 300,
2 TD, 2 int.

Receiving
San Francisco—Solomon, 4 for 52;
Clark, 4 for 45; Cooper, 2 for 15, 1 TD;
Wilson, 1 for 22; Young, 1 for 14; Pat-
ton, 1 for 6; Ring, 1 for 3.
Cincinnati—Ross, 11 for 104, 2 TD;
Collinsworth, 5 for 107; Curtis, 3 for
42; Kreider, 2 for 36; Johnson, 2 for 8;
Alexander, 2 for 3.

SUPER BOWL XVII

Washington 27, Miami 17
January 30, 1983 at Pasadena

Miami	7	10	0	0 —	17
Washington	0	10	3	14 —	27

Mia —Cefalo 76 pass from Woodley
(von Schamann kick)
Wash—FG Moseley 31
Mia —FG von Schamann 20
Wash—Garrett 4 pass from Theismann
(Moseley kick)
Mia —Walker 98 kickoff return
(von Schamann kick)
Wash—FG Moseley 20
Wash—Riggins 43 run (Moseley kick)
Wash—Brown 6 pass from Theismann
(Moseley kick)
Attendance—103,667

TEAM STATISTICS

	MIA	WASH
First downs	9	24
Rushing	7	14
Passing	2	9
By penalty	0	1
Total yardage	176	400
Net rushing yardage	96	276
Net passing yardage	80	124
Passes att.-comp. -had int.	17-4-1	23-15-1

Rushing

Miami—Franklin, 16 for 49; Woodley, 4 for 16; Nathan, 7 for 26; Harris, 1 for 1; Vigorito, 1 for 4.

Washington—Riggins, 38 for 166, 1 TD; Harmon, 9 for 40; Walker, 1 for 6; Theismann, 3 for 20; Garrett, 1 for 44.

Passing

Miami—Woodley, 4 of 14 for 97, 1 TD, 1 int; Strock, 0 of 3.

Washington—Theismann, 15 of 23 for 143, 2 TD, 2 int.

Receiving

Miami—Cefalo, 2 for 82, 1 TD; Harris, 2 for 15.

Washington—Brown, 6 for 60, 1 TD; Warren, 5 for 28; Walker, 1 for 27; Riggins, 1 for 15; Garrett, 2 for 13, 1 TD.

SUPER BOWL XVIII

LA Raiders 38, Washington 9
January 22, 1984, at Tampa

Washington	0	3	6	0 —	9
LA Raiders	7	14	14	3 —	38

LA —Jensen recovered blocked punt
in end zone (Bahr kick)
LA —Branch 12 pass from Plunkett
(Bahr kick)
Wash—FG Moseley 24
LA —Squirek 5 interception
(Bahr kick)
Wash—Riggins 1 run (kick blocked)
LA —Allen 5 run (Bahr kick)
LA —Allen 74 run (Bahr kick)
LA —FG Bahr 21
Attendance—72,920

TEAM STATISTICS

	WASH	LA
First downs	19	18
Rushing	7	8
Passing	10	9
By penalty	2	1
Total yardage	318	398
Net rushing yardage	90	231
Net passing yardage	193	154
Passes att.-comp -had int.	35-16-2	25-16-0

Rushing

Washington—Riggins, 16 for 64, 1 TD; Theismann, 3 for 18; J. Washington, 3 for 8.

LA Raiders—Allen, 20 for 191, 2 TD; King, 3 for 12; Hawkins, 3 for 6; Pruitt, 5 for 17; Plunkett, 1 for –2; Willis, 1 for 7.

Passing

Washington—Theismann, 16 of 35 for 243, 2 int.

LA Raiders—Plunkett, 16 of 25 for 172, 1 TD.

Receiving

Washington—Didier, 5 for 65; J. Washington, 3 for 20; Garrett, 1 for 17; Brown, 3 for 93; Biaquinto, 2 for 21; Monk, 1 for 26; Riggins, 1 for 1.

LA Raiders—Allen, 2 for 18; King, 2 for 8; Christensen, 4 for 32; Branch, 6 for 94, 1 TD; Hawkins, 2 for 20.

SUPER BOWL XIX

San Francisco 38, Miami 16
January 20, 1985, at Palo Alto

Miami	10	6	0	0 —	16
San Francisco	7	21	10	0 —	38

Mia— FG Von Schamann 37
SF —Monroe 33 pass from Montana (Wersching kick)
Mia— D. Johnson 2 pass from Marino (Von Schamann kick)
SF —Craig 8 pass from Montana (Wersching kick)
SF —Montana 6 run (Wersching kick)
SF —Craig 2 run (Wersching kick)
Mia— FG Von Schamann 31
Mia— FG Von Schamann 30
SF —FG Wersching 17
SF —Craig 16 pass from Montana (Wersching kick)
Attendance—84,059

TEAM STATISTICS	MIA	SF
First Downs	19	31
Rushing	2	16
Passing	17	15
By penalty	0	0
Total yardage	314	537
Net rushing yardage	25	211
Net passing yardage	289	326
Passes att.-comp.		
-had int.	50-29-2	35-24-0

Rushing
Miami—Nathan, 5 for 18; Bennett, 3 for 7; Marino, 1 for 0.
San Francisco—Tyler, 13 for 65; Montana, 5 for 59, 1 TD; Craig, 15 for 58, 1 TD; Harmon, 5 for 20; Solomon, 1 for 5; Cooper, 1 for 4.

Passing
Miami—Marino, 29 of 50, 318, 1 TD, 2 int.
San Francisco—Montana, 24 of 35 for 331, 3 TD.

Receiving
Miami—Nathan, 10 for 83; Clayton, 6 for 92; Rose, 6 for 73; D. Johnson, 3 for 28, 1 TD; Moore, 2 for 17; Cefalo, 1 for 14; Duper, 1 for 11.
San Francisco—Craig, 7 for 77, 2 TD; D. Clark, 6 for 77; Francis, 5 for 60; Tyler, 4 for 70; Monroe, 1 for 33; Solomon, 1 for 14.

SUPER BOWL XX

Chicago 46, New England 10
January 26, 1986, at New Orleans

Chicago	13	10	21	2 —	46
New England	3	0	0	7 —	10

NE —FG Franklin 36
Chi— FG Butler 28
Chi— FG Butler 24
Chi— Suhey 11 run (Butler kick)
Chi— McMahon 2 run (Butler kick)
Chi— FG Butler 24
Chi— McMahon 1 run (Butler kick)
Chi— Phillips 28 interception (Butler kick)
Chi— Perry 1 run (Butler kick)
NE —Fryar 8 pass from Grogan (Franklin kick)
Chi— Safety, Grogan tackled by Waechter in end zone
Attendance—73,818.

TEAM STATISTICS	CHI	NE
First downs	23	12
Rushing	13	1
Passing	9	10
By penalty	1	1
Total yardage	408	123
Net rushing yardage	167	7
Net passing yardage	241	116
Passes att.-comp.		
-had int.	24-12-0	36-17-2

Rushing
Chicago—Payton, 22 for 61; Suhey, 11 for 52, 1 TD; Gentry, 3 for 15; Sanders, 4 for 15; McMahon, 5 for 14, 2 TD; Thomas, 2 for 8; Perry, 1 for 1, 1 TD; Fuller, 1 for 1.
New England—Collins, 3 for 4; Weathers, 1 for 3; Grogan, 1 for 3; C. James, 5 for 1; Hawthorne, 1 for -4.

Passing
Chicago—McMahon, 12 of 20 for 256; Fuller, 0 of 4.
New England—Eason, 0 of 6; Grogan, 17 of 30 for 177, 2 int.

Receiving
Chicago—Gault, 4 for 129; Gentry, 2 for 41; Margerum, 2 for 36; Moorehead, 2 for 22; Suhey, 1 for 2; Thomas, 1 for 4.
New England—Morgan, 7 for 70; Starring, 2 for 39; Fryar, 2 for 24, 1 TD; Collins, 2 for 19; Ramsey, 2 for 16; C. James, 1 for 6; Weathers, 1 for 3.

Super Bowl Records

SERVICE
Most Games
5 Marv Fleming, Green Bay, I, II; Miami, VI, VII, VIII
 Larry Cole, Dallas, V, VI, X, XII, XIII
 Cliff Harris, Dallas, V, VI, X, XII, XIII
 D.D. Lewis, Dallas, V, VI, X, XII, XIII
 Preston Pearson, Baltimore, III; Pittsburgh, IX; Dallas, X,
 XII, XIII
 Charlie Waters, Dallas, V, VI, X, XII, XIII
 Rayfield Wright, Dallas, V, VI, X, XII, XIII
Most Games, Winning Team
4 By many players
Most Games, Coach
6 Don Shula, Baltimore, III; Miami, VI, VII, VIII, XVII, XIX
5 Tom Landry, Dallas, V, VI, X, XII, XIII
4 Harry (Bud) Grant, Minnesota, IV, VIII, IX, XI
 Chuck Noll, Pittsburgh, IX, X, XIII, XIV
Most Games, Winning Team, Coach
4 Chuck Noll, Pittsburgh, IX, X, XIII, XIV
2 Vince Lombardi, Green Bay, I, II
 Don Shula, Miami, VII, VIII
 Tom Landry, Dallas, VI, XII
 Tom Flores, Oakland/L.A. Raiders, XV, XVIII
 Bill Walsh, San Francisco, XVI, XIX

SCORING
POINTS
Most Points, Career
24 Franco Harris, Pittsburgh, 4 games (4-td)
22 Ray Wersching, San Francisco, 2 games (7-pat, 5-fg)
20 Don Chandler, Green Bay, 2 games (8-pat. 4-fg)
Most Points, Game
18 Roger Craig, San Francisco vs. Miami, XIX (3-td)
15 Don Chandler, Green Bay vs. Oakland, II (3-pat, 4-fg)

TOUCHDOWNS
Most Touchdowns, Career
- 4   Franco Harris, Pittsburgh, 4 games (4-r)
- 3   John Stallworth, Pittsburgh, 4 games (3-p)
  - Lynn Swann, Pittsburgh, 4 games (3-p)
  - Cliff Branch, Oakland/L.A. Raiders, 3 games (3-p)
  - Roger Craig, San Francisco, 1 game (1-r, 2-p)

Most Touchdowns, Game
- 3   Roger Craig, San Francisco vs. Miami, XIX (1-r, 2-p)
- 2   By 10 players

POINTS AFTER TOUCHDOWN
Most Points After Touchdown, Career
- 8   Don Chandler, Green Bay, 2 games (8 att)
  - Roy Gerela, Pittsburgh, 3 games (9 att)
  - Chris Bahr, Oakland/L.A. Raiders, 2 games (8 att)
- 7   Ray Wersching, San Francisco, 2 games (7 att)

Most Points After Touchdown, Game
- 5   Don Chandler, Green Bay vs. Kansas City, I (5 att)
  - Roy Gerela, Pittsburgh vs. Dallas, XIII (5 att)
  - Chris Bahr, L.A. Raiders vs. Washington, XVIII (5 att)
  - Ray Wersching, San Francisco vs. Miami, XIX (5 att)
  - Kevin Butler, Chicago vs. New England, XX (5 att)

FIELD GOALS
Field Goals Attempted, Career
- 7   Roy Gerela, Pittsburgh, 3 games
- 6   Jim Turner, N.Y. Jets-Denver, 2 games

Most Field Goals Attempted, Game
- 5   Jim Turner, N.Y. Jets vs. Baltimore, III
  - Efren Herrera, Dallas vs. Denver, XII

Most Field Goals, Career
- 5   Ray Wersching, San Francisco, 2 games (5 att)
- 4   Don Chandler, Green Bay, 2 games (4 att)
  - Jim Turner, N.Y. Jets-Denver, 2 games (6 att)
  - Uwe von Schamann, Miami, 2 games (4 att)

Most Field Goals, Game
- 4   Ray Wersching, San Francisco vs. Cincinnati, XVI
  - Don Chandler, Green Bay vs. Oakland, II

Longest Field Goal
- 48   Jan Stenerud, Kansas City vs. Minnesota, IV

SAFETIES
Most Safeties, Game
- 1   Dwight White, Pittsburgh vs. Minnesota, IX
  - Reggie Harrison, Pittsburgh vs. Dallas, X
  - Henry Waechter, Chicago vs. New England, XX

RUSHING

ATTEMPTS

Most Attempts, Career

- 101　Franco Harris, Pittsburgh, 4 games
- 64　John Riggins, Washington, 2 games

Most Attempts, Game

- 38　John Riggins, Washington vs. Miami, XVII

YARDS GAINED

Most Yards Gained, Career

- 354　Franco Harris, Pittsburgh, 4 games
- 297　Larry Csonka, Miami, 3 games

Most Yards Gained, Game

- 191　Marcus Allen, L.A. Raiders vs. Washingotn, XVIII
- 166　John Riggins, Washington vs. Miami, XVII

Longest Run from Scrimmage

- 74　Marcus Allen, L.A. Raiders vs. Washington, XVIII

TOUCHDOWNS

Most Touchdowns, Career

- 4　Franco Harris, Pittsburgh, 4 games
- 2　By 6 players

Most Touchdowns, Game

- 2　Elijah Pitts, Green Bay vs. Kansas City, I
  Larry Csonka, Miami vs. Minnesota, VIII
  Pete Banaszak, Oakland vs. Minnesota, XI
  Franco Harris, Pittsburgh vs. L.A. Rams, XIV
  Marcus Allen, L.A. Raiders vs. Washington, XVIII
  Jim McMahon, Chicago vs. New England, XX

PASSING

ATTEMPTS

Most Passes Attempted, Career
- 98 Roger Staubach, Dallas, 4 games
- 89 Fran Tarkenton, Minnesota, 3 games

Most Passes Attempted, Game
- 50 Dan Marino, Miami vs. San Francisco, XIX

COMPLETIONS

Most Passes Completed, Career
- 61 Roger Staubach, Dallas, 4 games
- 49 Terry Bradshaw, Pittsburgh, 4 games

Most Passes Completed, Game
- 29 Dan Marino, Miami vs. San Francisco, XIX

COMPLETION PERCENTAGE

Highest Completion Percentage, Career (40 attempts)
- 66.7 Joe Montana, San Francisco, 2 games (57-38)
- 63.6 Len Dawson, Kansas City, 2 games (44-28)

Highest Completion Percentage, Game (20 attempts)
- 73.5 Ken Anderson, Cincinnati vs. San Francisco, XVI (34-25)

HAD INTERCEPTED

Most Passes Had Intercepted, Game
- 4 Craig Morton, Denver vs. Dallas, XII

Most Passes Had Intercepted, Career
- 7 Craig Morton, Dallas-Denver, 2 games
- 6 Fran Tarkenton, Minnesota, 3 games

Most Attempts, Without Interception, Game
- 35 Joe Montana, San Francisco vs. Miami, XIX

TOUCHDOWN PASSES

Most Touchdown Passes, Career
- 9 Terry Bradshaw, Pittsburgh, 4 games
- 8 Roger Staubach, Dallas, 4 games

Most Touchdowns, Game
- 4 Terry Bradshaw, Pittsburgh vs. Dallas, XIII

PASS RECEIVING
RECEPTIONS
Most Receptions, Career
16   Lynn Swann, Pittsburgh, 4 games
15   Chuck Foreman, Minnesota, 3 games
Most Receptions, Game
11   Dan Ross, Cincinnati vs. San Francisco, XVI

YARDS GAINED
Most Yards Gained, Career
364   Lynn Swann, Pittsburgh, 4 games
268   John Stallworth, Pittsburgh, 4 games
Most Yards Gained, Game
161   Lynn Swann, Pittsburgh vs. Dallas, X
Longest Reception
80   Kenny King (from Plunkett), Oakland vs. Philadelphia, XV

TOUCHDOWNS
Most Touchdowns, Career
3   John Stallworth, Pittsburgh, 4 games
     Lynn Swann, Pittsburgh, 4 games
     Cliff Branch, Oakland/L.A. Raiders, 3 games
2   By 5 players
Most Touchdowns, Game
2   Max McGee, Green Bay vs. Kansas City, I
     Bill Miller, Oakland vs. Green Bay, II
     John Stallworth, Pittsburgh vs. Dallas, XIII
     Cliff Branch, Oakland vs. Philadelphia, XV
     Dan Ross, Cincinnati vs. San Francisco, XVI
     Roger Craig, San Francisco vs. Miami, XIX

INTERCEPTIONS BY
Most Interceptions by, Career
3   Rod Martin, Oakland, 1 game
     Chuck Howley, Dallas, 3 games
2   By 5 players
Most Touchdowns, Game
1   Herb Adderley, Green Bay vs. Oakland, II
     Willie Brown, Oakland vs. Minnesota, XI
     Jack Squirek, L.A. Raiders vs. Washingotn, XVIII
     Reggie Phillips, Chicago vs. New England, XX
Most Yards Gained, Career
75   Willie Brown, Oakland, 2 games
63   Chuck Howley, Dallas, 2 games
     Jake Scott, Miami, 3 games
Most Yards Gained, Game
75   Willie Brown, Oakland vs. Minnesota, XI
Longest Return
75   Willie Brown, Oakland vs. Minnesota, XI (TD)

KICKOFF RETURNS
Longest Kickoff Return
 98 Fulton Walker, Miami, XVII
Most Touchdowns, Career
 1 Fulton Walker, Miami, 2 games
Most Returns, Game
 7 Stephen Starring, New England vs. Chicago, XX

PUNTING
Longest Punt
 62 Rich Camarillo, New England vs. Chicago, XX
Highest Punting Average, Game (4 minimum)
48.5 Jerrel Wilson, Kansas City vs. Minnesota, IV

FUMBLES
Most Fumbles, Game
 3 Roger Staubach, Dallas vs. Pittsburgh, X
Most Fumbles Recovered, Game
 2 Jake Scott, Miami vs. Minnesota, VIII (1-own, 1-opp)
  Roger Staubach, Dallas vs. Pittsburgh, X (2-own)
  Randy Hughes, Dallas vs. Denver, XII (2-opp)
  Butch Johnson, Dallas vs. Denver, XII (2-own)
  Mike Singletary, Chicago vs. New England (2-opp)

150

About the Author

George Vecsey is a sports columnist with *The New York Times*. He has also covered such varied subjects as coal mining, religion, and city news for *The Times*, in addition to writing over a dozen books.

In 1976 Mr. Vecsey wrote the book *Loretta Lynn: Coal Miner's Daughter*, which became a best-seller and was made into the movie, *Coal Miner's Daughter*. Sissy Spacek won an Academy Award for her portrayal of Loretta Lynn.

In 1985 Mr. Vecsey helped write *Martina*, the autobiography of Martina Navratilova, the tennis star. That book was on the best-seller list for 10 weeks. He has also written *Five O'Clock Comes Early: A Young Man's Battle with Alcoholism*, with Bob Welch of the Los Angeles Dodgers. Recently, Mr. Vecsey was a co-author of *Sweet Dreams*, a novel based on the movie about Patsy Cline, starring Jessica Lange.

Among his other books are: *The Harlem Globe-trotters*, *Pro Basketball Champions*, and *Frazier/Ali*, all written for Scholastic; *One Sunset a Week: The Story of a Coal Miner; Getting Off the Ground; The Way It Was; Joy in Mudville; Young Sports Photographer with the Green Bay Packers;* and *The Bermuda Triangle: Fact or Fiction?*

Born in New York City, Mr. Vecsey attended Jamaica High School and Hofstra College, and worked for *Newsday* before joining *The New York Times* in 1968. From 1970 through 1972, he was the Appalachian correspondent for *The Times*, based in Louisville, Kentucky. In 1978 he covered the Papal Conclave in Rome and, in 1979, Pope John Paul's trips to Mexico and the United States.

George Vecsey lives in Port Washington, New York, with his wife, Marianne Graham Vecsey, an artist whose works are often shown in the New York area. They have three children: Laura, Corinna, and David.